ncw

c

D0298123

Like Angels Falling

By the same author

The Greenway

Cast the First Stone

Bird

Fade to Grey

Final Frame

The Angel Gateway

Like Angels Falling

Jane Adams

LIMERICK COUNTY LIBRARY
CHSS806
WITHDRAWN FROM STOCK

MACMILLAN

First published 2001 by Macmillan
an imprint of Macmillan Publishers Ltd
25 Eccleston Place, London SW1W 9NF
Basingstoke and Oxford
Associated companies throughout the world
www.macmillan.com

ISBN 0 333 90524 5 (hardback)
ISBN 0 333 90526 1 (trade paperback)

Copyright © Jane Adams 2001

The right of Jane Adams to be identified as the
author of this work has been asserted by her in accordance
with the Copyright, Designs and Patents Act 1988.

All rights reserved. No part of this publication may be
reproduced, stored in or introduced into a retrieval system, or
transmitted, in any form, or by any means (electronic, mechanical,
photocopying, recording or otherwise) without the prior written
permission of the publisher. Any person who does any unauthorized
act in relation to this publication may be liable to criminal
prosecution and civil claims for damages.

9 8 7 6 5 4 3 2 1

A CIP catalogue record for this book is available from
the British Library.

Typeset by SetSystems Ltd, Saffron Walden, Essex
Printed and bound in Great Britain by
Mackays of Chatham plc, Chatham, Kent

For my mother.
Thanks for all the stamps!
And for my sister-in-law Rowena,
the other trainee gardener.

Part One

Prologue

Since that day he had kept the curtains closed and blocked out the sun. At night, he opened the window and switched on the single light, a naked bulb suspended from an ornate rose in the centre of his room. He would lie on his bed and watch the moths fly in through the open window and circle frantically around the harsh, unshaded lamp until they fell with scorched and broken wings onto the wooden floor.

Like angels, he thought, like angels falling from the sky, as they had on that final, terrible day.

He could not re-create the images he'd seen, the ones the artist had painted on the vaulted ceiling and the curving walls. He had neither the means nor, at that time, the skill, though the images had burned so deep into his brain he need not even close his eyes to see them. But, instead of paint, he had the broken wings of his moths and pinned them lovingly to his bedroom walls, mimicking the visions of the falling angels, and his hand became the hand of God, pointing the way to their salvation, leading the way back to the burning, cleansing light.

There had been two survivors from that night. Two they knew about, that was.

The first was an old man, who had spilt what was left

of his life blood when they lifted the beam from his legs. The second was a five-year-old girl. She had been trapped under debris right at the centre of the house. They released her three hours after her world had blown itself apart and she had walked away, unmarked, a tiny figure in a short white nightgown, blonde hair falling to her waist.

She had rarely spoken since that night. They had called her Katie, Katie being the wife of the officer who had pulled her from the wreckage. They never knew her real name. The neighbours swore they'd not seen the child before and there had been little of a personal nature left inside the house. Everything that might give clues to identity had been burnt on a garden bonfire the afternoon before.

It was eleven years later, on a dull February day, when Katie walked into her foster mother's living room and spoke to her for the very first time.

'He's coming back,' she said.

Chapter One

The video was of a youngish man. George put him perhaps in his middle thirties, though he had an ageless look that could have meant anything from twenty-five to forty. It was a pleasing face, handsome in a boyish, not quite finished way, framed by a mane of untidy red hair. But it was the eyes that compelled attention. Deep, melting brown, with more than a trace of humour. The eyes and the sweet, self-deprecating smile.

The production values were first-rate, but the presentation was simple, almost basic. The young man sat in an old armchair. Off to one side, a picture window showed a view of open sea and clear blue sky. He smiled at his audience, eyes seeming to meet theirs, and he spoke softly, explaining as he must have done a thousand times.

'You know, it's all a matter of timing. If I'd been some young girl in the hills above Fatima or a cranky little thing fresh from the fields of Domrémy, come to lead the troops to victory, I'd probably be headed for sainthood by now.

'If I'd even been religious it would have helped. As it was, I was a half-grown, more-than-half-cynical kid, living on an anonymous, sprawling, concrete-infested estate on the outskirts of an equally uninspiring Midlands town. I just happened to look out of the wrong window at the wrong moment, and that was it. Life as I knew it chopped off in its prime, and no one had even asked me if I minded.

'I was fifteen years old at the time. Gangly, awkward, growing out of my body and prone to teenage spots and an over-endowment of grease in my hair. Just another kid, tortured by hormones and doing my best to escape the attentions of adults and the war games played by my peers.

'I didn't ask to see whatever it was I saw. True, in my heart of hearts I might have wanted to be different, to be marked out from the general herd in some way. But this way? This was the last way I'd have chosen and that's the truth of it.'

The man on the screen froze as George pressed pause on the remote control.

'The Prophet, Martyn Shaw,' he said.

'So-called prophet,' his companion said, nodding. 'You know much about him?'

George shook his head. 'Only what I've seen in the media. I know a branch of his order came under investigation, oh, a couple of years ago, something to do with insider dealing I believe, but I had no involvement in that.'

'The deaths, ten, eleven years ago. You heard about them?'

'Of course. The papers and the television were full of it.'

'Twelve dead. They blew themselves apart. And two others killed themselves last year.'

George frowned. Looking at his friend, he wondered where all of this was leading. 'If memory serves, this one,

Martyn Shaw, he took over after that, didn't he? Wasn't their original leader, Daniel Morgan, among the dead?'

'That was never proved. Some of the bodies were little more than fragments and they'd gone to great lengths to get rid of personal items. They'd posted what they claimed was a list of "the blessed", as they called their suicides, to *The Times*, but we know for a fact that it was falsified. Even the sex of the victims didn't match.'

'We?' George queried. 'Patrick, you've been retired three years now and I'd have been told if they'd recalled you. So who's "we"?'

Patrick sighed and reached for the remote to stop the video. 'Parents,' he said. 'We're parents. We formed a sort of support group about a year ago.' He glanced awkwardly at George. 'Well, Barbara joined it and I suppose I got dragged along if we're going to be accurate.'

'Your daughter?'

Patrick nodded. 'She went to one of their introductory things. Some meditation session they held at that place of theirs near Oakham. Went on the Friday night a normal, sane person and by Sunday she was one of them. We've barely seen her since, George. That was eighteen months ago. Babs is going frantic. Mitch writes, but she won't come home. She's even given up her job to go and work in one of their damned communes. We're at the end of our rope.'

He got up, scooping his whisky glass off the arm of his leather chair and crossing to the sideboard. He poured another, double measure, and gestured towards George. 'Refresh your glass?'

'No, no thank you. I'm fine. How old is Mitch, Patrick? It's been some time . . .'

His friend laughed shortly. 'Oh, no, you're not giving me that. Mitch is no baby, I know. She was twenty-four this year, but she's a naïve twenty-four. A mere kid.'

George nodded, considering. He had rarely seen Patrick so agitated. They had worked together both at the Home Office and in the Diplomatic Protection Group, but he'd not seen his friend and one-time colleague in well over a year, closer to two now he thought about it, and it occurred to him suddenly that Patrick had grown old. Patrick had passed through almost the same career route as George. Ex-army, transferring to the DPG, their paths diverging only when Patrick moved over to work for MI6 and George joined Eric Dignan and other members of the DPG in what Dignan affectionately called his Corporation – men and women drawn from all branches of the Service who acted as consultants and liaised between the different branches of British and overseas undercover operations. He had seen little of Patrick after that and even less since he retired.

George pressed play on the video recorder and the man on screen moved once more, gesturing with his left hand as though reaching out towards his audience.

'I'm not saying that this is the only way,' he continued. 'Perhaps, for many, it's not even going to be the right way, but what I am saying to you is this. Come to our meetings. Listen to what we have to say and see for yourself the happiness that belonging to our organization has brought to those who have chosen and who have been chosen.' He smiled again. 'I have to tell you, though, not everyone who wants to belong will be able to join us. We have turned away many who, in their deepest hearts, wanted to believe but didn't have quite what it takes to be one of us. To be the Eyes of God is a privilege and a joy, but it cannot be the way for everyone.'

Impatiently, Patrick switched off the tape. 'Sorry,' he said. 'Take it with you if you want to see more, but he makes my flesh crawl.'

'Good psychology, though,' George commented. 'Most churches just want bums on seats, they don't threaten their faithful with a selection process.'

'It's not a damned church,' Patrick told him angrily. 'It's a cult, a fad, a piece of propaganda designed to corrupt the innocent. Steal our children's minds.' He glanced at George as though suddenly embarrassed by his outburst.

'Is that what they say at this support group of yours?'

'Something like. And it's true, George. It's bloody true.'

George frowned slightly. From what he remembered of Mitch, she was not a young lady who had ever been weak-minded. Not especially innocent either, he thought, doing his best not to smile at the memory of catching a seventeen-year-old Mitch and her boyfriend in the back seat of her father's car. Mitch was normal, healthy, curious and very bright. 'I find it hard to think of Mitch being sucked into anything without thinking first,' he said. 'She was always so sharp.'

'We thought so too,' Patrick said sadly. 'We thought, it's just Mitch experimenting. Like that monastery thing.

You remember, she went on a retreat or whatever to that Taoist place. And when she joined those left-wing radical things in school.'

George smiled. 'It was CND, from what I remember. It's perfectly respectable, Patrick.'

'Whatever.' He shrugged uncomfortably. 'I mean, we expected a bit of rebellion. Kids nowadays. But we thought, breeding will out in the end. She came from a loving home, a good, solid background, and when she finally knuckled down and took herself off to college . . .'

'Oxford, wasn't it?' George asked.

'Yes. We thought, right, Mitch has got it all out of her system and she'll be fine now. Then this.'

He slumped back in his chair and downed the whisky in two gulps. George winced – it deserved better attention than that. It was warm in Patrick's library, a large fire burning in the grate. Logs from the coppice at the back of the house and he could smell applewood. Patrick had mentioned at dinner that a couple of the oldest trees had been grubbed out of the orchard this autumn. He got up and wandered over to the window, pulling back the heavy curtains to see if it was still snowing outside.

'I'm not sure what you want me to do, Patrick. You know I'm about to resign. It becomes official at the end of the month.'

'And that's exactly it. Oh, I've tried so-called official channels. Police don't want to be bothered.'

'Well, she is twenty-four.'

'I know, I know. And my erstwhile colleagues are no more help. Said it's out of their domain. They've got the usual monitors in place, but since he moved his main operation stateside, Martyn Shaw is, they said, no longer their concern.'

'So where do I come in?' George asked, though he thought he could already guess.

'Well, when I heard about you setting up on your own, I thought, ideal. One of us, able to act without all those damned restrictions.' He stood up and came over to join George by the window. 'Find the dirt on him, George. Show him for the complete charlatan he is. I can pay, of course. Whatever it takes, you know I'm good for it.' He sighed deeply and, now he stood closer, George could see clearly just how grey his skin had become. The reddened eyes from night after night of drinking.

'I'll see what I can do,' he said, wondering what his partner would make of it all.

Chapter Two

Outside it was snowing again, but the ground was too wet for it to settle and already the streets were covered in a yellowish greasy slush. Snow, Ray Flowers thought, shouldn't be allowed in cities. All it did was get dirty.

February had never been a favourite month but this one was proving to be better than most. He leaned back against the wide sill of the big bay window and surveyed his new domain with great satisfaction. He'd been doubtful when George had first brought him to see this place, fearing it was too far from the centre of town and too expensive but, now that they were finally installed and the brass plaque was on the massive green front door he could see that George had been right. First floor of a large Victorian house, long since converted. Below there was a solicitor, above them an accountant's office (Ray had already enquired about terms and been shocked by the estimate), with Flowers-Mahoney Executive Security and Investigations now sandwiched in between.

We need to make a statement, George had told him. Show that we're not some twopenny-halfpenny firm dealing in divorce cases and cheap alarm systems. We need an address. And boy did they have one now – Clarendon Park, at the Stoneygate end – and the bills to prove it. Now all he had to do was master the damned computer.

Sarah came in carrying mugs of tea. She set them

down on Ray's new desk and smiled at him. 'You look pleased with yourself.'

'I am. I actually think this might work.'

'Course it will. You and George, all the experience you have between you, not to mention the deviousness and the bloody-mindedness, how could it fail?'

She came over and lay a cool long-fingered hand against his cheek before leaning forward to kiss him. Ray smiled back at her.

It was a lopsided clownish smile these days, inhibited by the scars that criss-crossed his cheek and deformed one side of his mouth. Ray had never been what you might call handsome, but the petrol bomb attack which had left his face and hands laced with burn scars had put paid to any faint illusion he might ever have had. A year ago he had been a policeman. DI Flowers, twenty-odd years in Her Majesty's service. A year ago he'd been in hospital, not sure if he wanted to live or die, but life, he reflected, has a way of throwing the unexpected in a person's way. And a year ago he had not had Sarah Gordon.

She had a mane of warm red hair, large grey eyes that could be hard as granite or soft as river water depending on her mood, and an intelligent humour that so often made him laugh or put him in his place. Happiness had come late into Ray Flowers's life but now that it had he was determined to drink in every moment of it.

Ashenfield was a category-A prison, or at least it had a category-A wing which effectively put the whole estate under the same regime. It was modern, built square around a block-paved courtyard and utterly characterless. Three sides of the quadrangle were single-storeyed, the fourth was topped off by the offices which housed the administration staff and the infirmary with its four-bedded ward and its side room for high-risk prisoners who must be separated from the rest.

Harrison Lee was dying. He knew it. The doctor said that he was merely sick, pneumonia following a dose of flu that had left him weak and vulnerable to infection. They had treated his illness and it had responded. Harrison Lee had not.

He had been at Ashenfield for almost the past two years. Before that he had inhabited half a dozen other jails, some for a few weeks, others for many months, but two years was the longest anywhere.

Because of its height, the infirmary actually had a view. Last night Harrison Lee could see stars, though tonight the clouds had gathered and thickened into a blanket filled with snow and yellowed by the sodium lights that marked the perimeter fence. He had lain and watched it fall for almost an hour.

Lee was in pain. He had pretended to be asleep when the nurse had come in with his last medication and they had not bothered to wake him, thinking that he would buzz if he wanted something. The staff were conscientious here. Calm, efficient and unquestioning, seeing him only as a sick old man, not as the animal the world judged him to be. But the pain was bad now, air rasping in raw lungs and pressure sores on his thin buttocks and bony shoulders adding to his discomfort. He no longer had the strength to turn himself.

He closed his eyes, knowing that time was short. That he must do what he had to do before the last medication rounds at ten, when they would be certain to wake him in order to give him the sleeping pill and the painkillers that had become his nightly routine. Concentration did not come easily these days. Tricks of the mind that he had once achieved almost without thought were now only memories.

Eyes closed, he slowed his laboured breathing, trying to ease each breath in and out of scarred lungs in an even ebb and flow, allowing his pulse rate to fall to almost nothing as his muscles relaxed, becoming so heavy that there was no movement left in them.

He stilled his thoughts, concentrating only on the breath, the drawing in and releasing of life, his mind focused on that single point just above his diaphragm where the energy gathered and body linked to soul.

How difficult it was. Something he had done since childhood now took so much effort that the thought broke through that he might not succeed.

He began again, focusing once more on the gathering energy. He imagined himself floating above the limp, almost unconscious body, then pushing that energy outwards, towards the window, out of the window, floating high above the guards and the wire and the patrolling dogs, hovering above the white of fresh-fallen snow.

The city was a distant glow close to the horizon and he directed his consciousness towards it. In his mind he held the image of a single face and he imagined himself flying towards it, knowing that wherever that man might be he would find him. One man concealed in a city of thousands . . .

Harrison Lee died just before ten on 18 February. When the nurse entered his room, Lee's face was grey, all life and colour drained, though his body was still warm and it was clear he had been dead for only the shortest time. His thin hands were clawed against the blankets.

His death, thought the prison medical officer, might warrant a paragraph or two in the national papers. Much more probably in the local ones, as this place was uncomfortably close to where Lee had committed his crimes, and memories here were long and still filled with pain.

There would be many out there who wanted him dead and would be celebrating. Not a few who would have liked a hand in getting him that way.

Chapter Three

On 19 February George Mahoney travelled to London to see Eric Dignan and formalize his resignation. His tenure with the Corporation would end with the month but George had, as was usual practice in the department, been slowly phased from duty the moment he had announced his intention to leave. This meeting should have been a simple matter of telling his superiors he had not changed his mind, with a reminder from them that he still had a responsibility under the Official Secrets Act not to discuss his employment, even with his new partners.

'Patrick's been on to us,' Dignan said, surprising him.

'Yes, he told me,' George returned.

Dignan had been his boss for the past five years. Patrick's too, at one time.

'We directed him to you. Told him you were free-lancing.'

'So that's how he heard.' George took in the implications as he sipped his coffee. It was Colombian, good and strong. 'I wasn't aware that I was freelancing,' he said. 'I was under the impression that I had gone into business for myself.'

Dignan smiled at him. 'We'll pay you a retainer, George. And you can submit your expenses on the usual forms.'

George frowned. 'So what did Patrick say to you that he didn't tell me?'

'Coincidence of interest, that's all,' Dignan said shortly. 'It seems a stupid waste of personnel for us to duplicate the investigation. The Eyes of God are not your usual run-of-the-mill bunch of religious fanatics. They're mostly professionals, skilled people, highly educated like Patrick's daughter.' Dignan passed a manila folder across the desk. 'Take a look at it on your way home. Bank details still the same, are they?'

'And your interest is?'

'They've made some interesting investments, been unusually successful.'

'Insider trading?'

'Nothing we could prove, and frankly, George, I don't see that as our concern. What interests me more is what they do with their money. They're financing research into some pretty sensitive areas. They have major share holdings in two companies supplying parts for the European space programme and they've assisted with passage and papers for a number of scientists from the old Soviet bloc. All very much above board, but interesting none the less. And they've been pumping money into one of the biggest producers of synthetic diamonds. Happens to be in Kiev. Again, they're perfectly open about it all, publish twice-yearly audits carried out by an independent accountant . . .'

George smiled. 'And we're always suspicious of anyone who looks too honest.'

'Rare commodity, George. As you well know.'

'I know they own property. That the Eyes have spent money on that place out at Oakham.'

'Yes, and similar communities scattered around the country. Actually, they all seem to be pretty much self-supporting. Most of the membership work and they run courses from March to October. Meditation weekends and the like, which no doubt they charge a fortune for. And, to be fair, the children who want to go on to university or these namby-pamby training courses the government keeps setting up, the Eyes fund them to the hilt. None of their children come out with a BA and a mountain of debt, but it makes me wonder, George. And yes, I am suspicious of people who wear their hearts on their sleeves and their money bags open. When Daniel Morgan and Harrison Lee were in charge, the organization looked squeaky clean and we all know how that ended. This new man, Martyn Shaw, we know he was a protégé of Lee's and in my book that taints him. A dozen people dead last time.'

George frowned, remembering something that Patrick had mentioned. 'Patrick said there might have been other deaths?'

Dignan shook his head. 'A young couple died just over a year ago after they'd been to a meeting at the Oakham house. Sommers, I believe they call it. They left a note which blamed just about every influence they'd ever had on their lives. Parents, teachers, doctors and of course the Eyes of God, who'd apparently rejected them in some way.'

George nodded, remembering the video and Martyn Shaw's assertion that not everyone could make the grade.

'Turns out they both had a history of mental health problems. They'd met in a drug rehabilitation centre. The people out at Sommers House had alerted the local police when they'd turned up there stoned and tried to detain them until the police arrived. They got wind of what was going on and left. That night they overdosed, some sort of suicide pact apparently. No indication at all from the police investigation that those at Sommers had acted any way but properly.'

'But Patrick won't see that.'

'Patrick is emotionally involved. Of course he won't.'

George walked back along Charing Cross Road deep in thought, manila folder tucked inside his briefcase. He would have to tell Ray and he had informed Dignan of that. To his surprise, his request had not been denied, which meant the department already had a reason for wanting Ray involved.

'Ray knows about these people,' Dignan had said cryptically as George left. 'You ask him about the last time.'

The income would be useful, George thought, and Dignan would no doubt use whatever information he and Ray generated with or without their knowledge or permission, so they might as well get paid for it.

Sarah was having a house-warming party that evening and George had promised to be there. She had bought a tiny little place out at Peatling Magna, an eighteenth-century tied cottage with a small kitchen and disproportionately enormous garden. The garden, George guessed, was really for the benefit of Ray, who, much to everyone's surprise, had developed a passion for growing things over the last six months or so. He wondered how long it would be before Ray and Sarah finally capitulated and moved in together, instead of keeping up the pretence that Ray sometimes went home to the little flat next to their new office. He wondered also when Ray would decide what to do with the little place his aunt had left him the year before. Ray had talked about settling there for a while, and the cottage was close enough to commute, but in reality he seemed reluctant either to live there or to sell, stemming from his conviction that the place was haunted in some way. George had never thought of his friend as credulous, but where the cottage was concerned he was all but immovable.

A young girl followed him onto the platform of the underground station. She had dark eyes, black almost, in a pale face and thin brown hair that just reached her shoulders and hadn't been washed in days.

'Can you help me? Spare a little change? I'm trying to get money for the night shelter. I wouldn't bother you otherwise.'

George glanced at her, taking in the worn denim jeans and thin jacket, the 'Heroin Chic' too real for any catwalk, and he shook his head. 'No change,' he said, digging in the pocket of his coat. 'Oh, wait a minute.' He fished an unexpected twenty pence from the corner and handed it to her, taking no notice of her thanks. She moved away, trying her spiel on another as George hurried along the platform, trying not to think how much she reminded him of his daughter Jan.

*

LIMERICK COUNTY LIBRARY
H SS 806

In Mallingham at seven thirty and already winter dark, Ian Thomason set off for home. He had been playing at his best friend's house. It was only five doors away from his own home and he was eight years old, so, despite the cold and dark, no one saw any problem in him running back alone along the terraced street.

The boy was slightly built and blond, his hair copper-green in the glare of the streetlights. A mere five front doors and four entranceways between the closing of one home and the safety of another. It was nothing and it was everything. As he hurried by the third entranceway something moved in the deeper shadows between the houses.

Ian was startled and jumped back.

'Who's there?'

He stood still and then glanced round at his friend's house door. The mother had wanted to stand on the doorstep and watch him home, but Ian had insisted that he'd be all right. He wished now that he had let her and thought of going back, knowing that she'd walk him home if he asked her, but afraid it would make him look small and stupid.

He hesitated. He could see nothing in the shadow of the wall and he knew how dark the alleys got at night. You could imagine anything happening in them.

Telling himself not to be silly, he circled around the streetlight, stepping out onto the road away from the alley, ready to make a run for it to his own front door. Then the blackness in the deeper shadow moved again.

*

Harrison Lee was cremated on 20 February. There had been no announcement of the funeral in the press and the notice of his death had been delayed until the hastily arranged service was over. Feelings still ran high in the local area and the authorities would have been happier if he could have been cremated elsewhere, but he had no family and it had fallen to the state to dispose of him. Such niceties as location were therefore not taken into account.

A young man watched as the funeral party entered the crematorium. There were few mourners. Prison officials, a local minister, one of the prison visitors who had numbered Lee among his responsibilities. That was all. A man who had once wielded such power, now forgotten.

The young man stood next to a motorbike whose red and chrome trim gleamed in the winter sun. It was a vintage machine but designed for the racetrack rather than the road, with its café-racer styling and dropped bars. As distinctive as its black-clad owner.

The service was not long. Fifteen minutes at most. No one had a lot to say about the man who had died and those things they wished to say would have meant speaking ill of the dead. The service, therefore, was mostly silent and no one was sorry when it came to an end.

As the group came out, shaking hands, preparing to go their separate ways, the young man moved too. He glanced sideways at the two graves closest to him. Both children, commemorated by low white stones and fresh flowers, even after a dozen years. Roger Joyce, age nine, sleeping with the angels. Phillip Abrahams, age ten, beloved son. It seemed blasphemous that Lee's ashes would be scattered here.

The young man walked to his bike and glanced one last time over his shoulder at the departing officials before kicking the engine into life. The crack of straight-through pipes shattered the peace. The funeral party stared after him, appalled at this breach of silence, watching the offender ride away. A black-clad figure on a red and chrome machine.

Chapter Four

On the morning of 21 February George travelled to Sommers House to visit Mitch. Sommers was an Edwardian place set back in its own grounds and situated a few miles from Oakham on the Cottesmore road. It was built of the soft local stone with a Collyweston slate roof, deep grey in the dull February light and, George noted, sporting far more moss than was good for it. The gates stood open at the end of the drive and he turned his car towards the house, pulling up outside of the dark blue door. There were three men at work in the garden, rebuilding a low wall that separated a formal garden from the children's play area. The garden backed onto woodland – birch and oak from the shape of the naked trees and the last unfallen leaves. A pleasant spot, secluded and sheltered. It reminded him forcibly of the house not twenty miles from here where Mitch had spent her childhood years.

One of the men detached himself from the others and strolled over to George. He was dressed for work in tough boots and faded jeans. A baggy sweater finished the ensemble. It was dirtied with a rime of earth and moss from hefting the stones and the hand he held out towards George was grained with dirt and bleeding at the knuckles.

George shook it anyway. The grip was strong and

confident and the smile made the man's eyes crinkle pleasantly. He was not young, George thought, though he had been lifting the stones as though he still had a young man's strength.

'Bryn Jones,' the man introduced himself. 'You must be George Mahoney. Mitch is expecting you. In fact I think she's rather pleased, even if her father did send you.'

George laughed. 'I should really have come a long time ago,' he said. 'Mitch and I were good friends once. It shouldn't have taken Patrick to make me realize that.'

The door opened then and Mitch herself came bounding down the steps and hugged him with the enthusiasm he remembered of old. 'Come in, come in. Meet everyone. Oh, George, it's so good to see you.'

'Even if your father sent me?'

Mitch laughed. 'Even if. How is he? How's Mum? Come on in.'

It was not the kind of welcome he had expected. He had, at the very least, expected to be welcomed with more reserve. His notion of religious cults was that they didn't encourage outsiders, and certainly didn't invite them in for tea.

There were several people at work in the large kitchen, obviously preparing lunch.

'You will stay?' Bryn asked him.

'I'd love to if it's not going to cause trouble.'

'None at all.' A red-haired woman came over to greet him. Her hair was greying at the temples and she looked to be of a similar age to Bryn. Fifty perhaps, George thought. 'I'm Irene,' she said. 'Bryn's wife. And there'll be fifteen of us at lunch, so one more will make no difference at all.'

They were a lively bunch and they made tea the way he liked it. Leaves instead of bags and good and strong. He couldn't help feeling that they were vetting him, ensuring that he was not going to upset Mitch in any way before they allowed him to be alone with her. But he couldn't blame them, he supposed. He would have done the same for a member of his own household. Not, he thought sadly, that he had one any more.

After half an hour he sensed that they were satisfied and asked Mitch to show him around the grounds. They circled the house slowly, admiring the landscape, and Mitch proudly pointed out the changes that had been made in the five years the group had lived there.

'We've replanted the orchard,' she said. 'Kept what old trees still gave fruit and grubbed out the rest. We've replanted with old varieties, apples, pears, plums, and of course it's all organic. We grow most of our own vegetables. You should see the size of the freezers Irene's got in the cellar.'

'Irene does most of the cooking then?'

Mitch laughed. 'Irene knows most. She supervises and the rest of us work on a rota.'

'How many live here? Irene mentioned fifteen for lunch.'

'There are twenty-two altogether. Some have jobs away from home and we have ten children on the site. The youngest was born here. Elaine went into labour early and didn't quite make it to the hospital.'

'You still believe in all that then? Work, hospitals, doctors . . .'

Mitch laughed at him. 'Oh, George, what do you think we are here? The Prophet teaches that we should take the best of the old, the best of the new and keep knowledge alive and growing.'

George smiled at her. 'I don't know what you're like, Mitch. You'll have to teach me.' He paused, looking obediently at the old roses that Mitch assured him would be spectacular in June. 'You do seem happy though,' he conceded.

'And will you tell my father that?'

'I can tell him. He won't believe me. He feels it, you know, not seeing you. And he's drinking rather more than is good for him.'

'I'm sorry for that. I truly am. But they could see me any time. They could drive over, just as you did. Stay for lunch, spend time meeting the others. I've told them that, but they just won't come here.'

'Knowing your father, does that surprise you?'

Mitch shook her head. 'George, I call them twice a week. I write. I tell them what I'm doing here. I tell them about my work, but they won't come here and I don't want to go home.'

'Afraid they might convince you to stay if you did?'

'A bit of me is afraid they might force me to if I did.'

'Force you?'

'Oh, come on George, don't go all innocent on me. They wouldn't be the first desperate parents to pay a fortune for someone to deprogramme their kid. But I'm not a kid any more. I'm my own person and I'm happy here.'

They walked in silence through the formal gardens at the back of the house and George commented on how well tended everything was.

Mitch nodded. 'We've got a couple of very gifted garden designers on the team. They take outside projects too and the rest of us are rosta'd for weeding, grass cutting and the rest. I just do my basic couple of hours a week, but those more into gardening choose to do almost all of their duty time in the gardens.'

'Duty time?'

She grinned at him. 'A place like this doesn't run itself and in the conference season it's really hectic. This time of year, though, it belongs to the family and it's really peaceful.'

'The family? You think of these people that way?'

'Yes, I do. I love my parents, George, but I've always needed more affection than Dad knows how to give. And Mum, well, I've never really known what to make of her and the feeling's mutual, you know that.'

Knowing Mitch's parents, George felt he couldn't argue. 'They love you,' he said finally.

'I know they do. I know.'

There was a moment of discomfort between them. George let it sit for a while and then asked, 'How many work outside?'

'Most of us, at least part-time. There are a handful of people who concentrate on running this place day-to-day and they do the bulk of the cooking, but we're all expected to help and we have a couple of part-time staff for the pre-school kids. We used outside help till we got our own trained. The older ones go off to school as usual. In the summer, when people come for meditational retreats and such, we run a crèche and hire staff as we need from one of the agencies.'

'And you? Your father said you'd given up your job.'

Mitch laughed again. 'Which job? As of a week ago I was working as an analyst at a biochemical company in Peterborough, but I've just landed something much better.'

'Oh?'

'Next month I'm off to Cambridge. I've got a research fellowship. Pay's not good but it's the first step on a really big ladder. Biotechnology, exactly the field I trained for.'

'I'm happy for you, Mitch, I really am. Will that mean you have to move away?'

'I've got lodgings for the week with family friends of Bryn and Irene. People they knew before they came here. And yes, we do still keep in touch with non-members. I'll drive back at weekends. The community is helping me to buy a car. It's a cut in wages, so I won't be able to contribute as much, but everyone's so pleased for me.'

'And there's no problem with you moving away like that? Aren't they worried you might not come back?'

Mitch stopped walking and turned to face him. 'Look, George, I know you're here with the best of intentions, but listen to me. This isn't some closed-door cult. When we join this chapter, or any of the others around the country, we make a commitment to the community and yes, most of what we earn goes into the community.'

'Ah. I wondered when we would get to the money side.'

'Enough, George. We all get to keep a good portion of what we earn. Families get to keep more, of course, because their kids need things that the community can't provide. School trips, fashionable clothes, all the growing-up things that kids need these days. We keep our private bank accounts and have the freedom to spend our own money any way we please, and when we need something extra, like I need a car, the community helps with it.

'We've no other commitments. No food to buy or rent to pay. But the most important thing is this. If I woke up tomorrow morning and decided this wasn't for me, there's a gate over there to which we all have keys and I could pack my stuff and go. I wouldn't even have to say goodbye if I didn't want.'

'Can you be sure of that?'

'Yes. Yes, I can. Two people left last year. I can give you their addresses if you like. I still write to both of them and they write back. We don't want people here who can't give 100 per cent of themselves. As the Prophet says, not everyone can make the grade. There's still work for people to do, even on the outside.'

'And those who don't fit in any longer, Mitch? Are they told to leave?'

She shook her head vehemently. 'It isn't like that,' she said. 'People make up their own minds if they want to stay or go.'

'But not everyone can join in the first place, can they? What's the selection procedure? How was it decided, for instance, that you belonged here?'

'The Prophet spoke to me,' Mitch said softly, 'and I listened to what he had to say.'

George spent the afternoon at Sommers House and left only after the evening meal was over and he was told gently that the meeting time that followed was a private affair.

'You are more than welcome to stay,' Bryn told him. 'Feel free to wander round the house or the gardens until we finish. We meditate together for about an hour and then discuss any business that the chapter might have.'

'Chapter?' George enquired. It was the second time he had heard the community spoken of in that way.

'Like the Hell's Angels,' Mitch said, grinning at him. 'Yeah, I know, bad joke, though Bryn ought to own up that he was the first to make it.'

Bryn smiled back at her. 'The Prophet says that we are chapters in the book of life,' he said. 'That we all go to make the full story.'

George decided he would leave. It was a long drive home and he felt he ought to call in and see Patrick on the way. He told Mitch so.

'Tell them what you've seen here,' Mitch said. 'That I'm happy and I'm working hard at my career. That I'm not brainwashed or locked away, and that we'd all love it if they'd come over.'

As George drove away, most of the community stood

waving on the step, the children chasing after the car until their parents called them back.

He could understand why Mitch wanted to belong here. It was, in its way, the perfect solution for her. A place to belong with enough freedom that she could feel master of her own destiny, enough restriction to make her feel secure.

He doubted Patrick would see any of it that way. Like George, Patrick had seen too much of the world not to be wary of perfection.

Chapter Five

It was dark by the time Ray reached Mallingham and parked in a side street close to St Leonard's Church. St Leonard's was Victorian Romanesque, with a rounded apse and an ugly 1960s hall tacked on the side, reached through the vestry. When Ray had first visited the church it had been surrounded by narrow terraced streets, but now it stood alone, the final outpost of what had once been a community but was now merely a central island in a sea of rubble.

The vicarage had been demolished the year before, Ray remembered reading in the papers. There had been a general protest about its destruction. Victorian, like its church, but with an interior remodelled in the Art Nouveau style, complete with a spectacular stained-glass window above the main staircase and a depiction of the four seasons in decorated tiles on the oak fire surround of the drawing room.

Ray had been there once, with the friend he had come to see. The local protest had at least meant the rescue of some of the more spectacular décor. It had been bought by a local reclamation yard and Ray had amused himself imagining the stained glass and nubile young women representing spring and autumn decorating the hall of some modern semi.

Inside St Leonard's the oak pews were gone, together

with the pulpit and the altar. The space that had once been occupied now yawned empty. A handful of volunteers were sorting clothes and stuffing them into bin liners. Martha, they told him, was in the hall and he should go on through.

The church hall had once been a community centre, used for youth clubs and pre-school playgroups. A new leisure centre had been built about a mile away and now those groups had migrated to it, leaving only the bare basketball hoops and the scuffed markings of the court on the stained floor. Two of the windows were still painted with Disney animals and the walls were stained with tiny, grubby handprints and fingerprints of red paint. The smell in the room reminded Ray forcibly of school dinners – how many years ago . . . don't even ask – the faint scent of cabbage that lingered long after the vegetable and the peculiar odour of stale gravy mingled with the richer saucy aroma of baked beans.

Martha was serving, her customers lined up beside the trestle tables. She didn't have room or permission to sleep them here, but Ray knew that she often bent the rules when the one small local hostel was full. Martha had a single-mindedness that was difficult to resist. It had been almost a year since he had last seen her. He had been in hospital at the time and too sick to take much notice of her being there, but she had come because he needed friends in his time of crisis and he had been drawn here tonight for much the same reason.

The notice of Harrison Lee's death in the local paper had brought the memories back with a painful exactitude that only someone who shared them would understand.

He knew that Martha would have felt the same and that she would have need of him.

There was no surprise when she saw him, only a quick smile that lifted her face from the ordinary. She had changed her hair, Ray noticed, had it straightened – relaxed, didn't they call it? – and it was fastened at her neck by a coloured slide.

'I need someone to pour tea, Ray,' she called out to him. 'Rowena, set him on, will you, darling? Your hands all right for that?'

'I'm sure I can manage,' Ray said.

Rowena smiled at him uncertainly, her gaze taking in the scarred face and awkward hands, clearly not quite comfortable with making him work. But she sorted him out with the tea urn and then went back to serving, glancing anxiously at him from time to time as though the task might prove too much.

It was twenty minutes before Martha had finished and beckoned him away.

She led him through into a small office behind the vestry. It was empty but for an old table and a couple of wooden chairs. A telephone stood on the desk beside a card index file and a framed photograph. The walls were plastered with pictures. Children, the elderly, men and women of every age between. Some had brief descriptions written beneath and locations, where and how they had last been seen. Each had been given a number relating to the index file. Ray had been only a sergeant when Martha first began this project with nothing more than a tele-phone and a handful of index cards, but it was no surprise to him that she was still involved. Once Martha got the bit between her teeth no one could stop her.

She knew why he had come.

'I'm glad he's dead,' she told Ray. 'But what he stood for isn't dead. It just goes on getting stronger. And now their so-called Prophet's supposed to be coming over for another lecture tour this summer. He should be banned from the country, Ray. Him and all his sort.'

Ray nodded, more in sympathy than agreement. 'There's nothing to connect him to Harrison Lee and what he did,' he said softly.

'Nothing but what they're both a part of. That so-called religion of theirs. You know as well as I do, Lee would have taken over from Morgan if the law hadn't caught up with him. Daniel Morgan killed himself rather than face the music and he named this Martyn Shaw to take over from him. That speaks for itself.'

Ray felt that he had to defend Shaw. 'And the new organization has done everything it can to separate itself from the past, Martha.'

'Others have died. You can't deny that.'

'When Lee was arrested, yes.'

'They weren't the only ones. Two suicides last year. Morgan poisoned their minds and you can't tell me this new one hasn't done the same.'

Ray sighed but knew it was no good arguing. Martha had every reason for hatred and nothing he could say or do would alter that. Morgan had been insane. There was no real doubt about that. He'd believed in his own power, talked about raising a new ... what had he called it?

Something like a messiah but that wasn't the word he used. Ray couldn't recall now. Lee had been involved in Morgan's schemes, though there had been signs of a split between them. It had never been clear what this was about and Lee had never elaborated.

'He still has his followers,' Martha said quietly.

'Who? Morgan?'

'No. I mean that creature Lee. They keep separate from the rest. Pretend not to believe in this Shaw, but it's all one.' She looked up at him and her dark eyes filled with tears. 'I'm afraid it's all going to start again,' she said. 'Who knows what Lee told his people to do once he was dead. He vowed, Ray. Vowed in court that he'd come back and finish things.'

Ray pulled her close and held her tight. 'He's dead, Martha. What more can he do now?' But his gaze fell on the framed photograph sitting on the desk. The picture of a nine-year-old boy with a bright smile and tight, close-cropped curls. Ray stared at it and knew that there were scars not even time could heal.

Katie was not unhappy at home, nor did she want to upset her foster parents. She had lived with them since a month after the explosion and, to her, Guy and Lisa Fellows were Mum and Dad, and their son, Gavin, only in fact a few months younger, was her brother.

She had, naturally enough, thought a lot about the events that had taken place before, but for the most part they were misty and vague and full of an unease that, even as a teenager and far removed in time, she found uncomfortable to dwell upon. She had become part of the Fellows family to such an extent that no one really talked about the time before. That people meeting the family for the first time assumed that she and Gavin must be twins, being so close in age. Assuming too that Katie, like Gavin, must be deaf, as the natural language used between them was almost always sign.

This had been a major factor in Katie's settling with the Fellows. Even eleven years on, Katie still did not like to speak. It wasn't that she couldn't, it wasn't even that she didn't want to communicate, as the lively signed conversations she had with her family testified. And it wasn't that she felt she had secrets to hide that might be prised from her if she began to talk. It was more fundamental than that. Someone long ago had told Katie to be silent and Katie found it hard to break that commandment.

Sometimes, in the quiet of her own room, she practised. She would look into the mirror and force her lips into the shapes the words should make. It was a private ritual she had gone through ever since she had come to live with the Fellowses and one she wished with all her heart that she could share. She had an innate sense that it was important to keep alive her ability to speak, even if she rarely used it. The command had been in place, iron-bound and immutable, until the dreams began and everything in her life turned upside-down.

And now Katie could resist this new command no longer. There was someone she had to find. A new threat had arisen that she knew instinctively was linked to the events of eleven years before and a return of the old fears that had once visited her nightmares and woken her, screaming with terror.

On the night of 21 February Katie ran away from home. She didn't want to go and she didn't know why she was being made to leave, but the utter compulsion was far too much for her to resist. Earlier that day she had found for the first time that permission had been given to break the silence and the knowledge was terrifying in its implications. 'He's coming back,' Katie had told her mother, 'coming back.' But she was unable to name the man whose face she saw, his features painted so clearly on her mind's eye that she did not even need to close her eyes to see. Something bad was about to happen and Katie had to stop it, though how she could even begin to convey that to her mum and dad was beyond her.

Instead, she crept from their house a little after midnight, leaving behind a letter that explained as best she could, together with an apology for borrowing the £50 emergency money that her father always kept in the house. There was only one solution that Katie could see. She had to follow the dream, and in the dream she had seen the face of a second man, more elusive and fragmentary, his image sitting stubbornly at the edges of her consciousness as though the other one, the one she feared, was trying to push him away.

He was the key to this, she decided. The key to the bad thing. The one who had the answers and could make the evil stop.

Katie didn't know for certain where to find him and had no idea who he was, but she knew that she had to try. *He* was coming back, he had work to finish, and Katie knew that he would be looking for her.

The Prophet Martyn Shaw had been on retreat, meditating. His seclusion meant that the news of Lee's death was close on seventy-two hours old by the time his second-in-command, Charles Marriott, gave it to him. He took it calmly, though Marriott could see the tension in the Prophet's slim body and the tightening of the mouth that he had come to associate with great inner turmoil closely confined.

'Do we know who he chose?' Shaw asked. 'He left no will?'

Marriott shook his head. 'He left no words, but we know what he planned, Martyn.'

The Prophet nodded slowly. 'I've dreaded this,' he said quietly.

'There's more,' Marriott told him. 'Katie ran away from home last night.'

Shaw gave him a sharp look. 'We've someone looking out for her, I hope?'

'Taken care of. We've had her watched ever since we heard Lee was weakening. Best-protected runaway any-where.' He smiled, trying to lighten the mood, but Shaw did not respond, his mind on other children whose faces he could not yet see and whose names he did not yet know but who would be dead before the month was through.

The young man's hair was as dark as his clothing and, as he crossed the wasteground behind St Leonard's Church, only his pale face reflected what little light penetrated this far from the deserted road. He moved slowly, careful of the piled rubbish and partly demolished walls, the unexpected holes where garden drains had once been and the kitchen steps that led out into now-blasted yards. He knew this place well enough. It had been in this condition for the past two years, since the development money dried up and the land was abandoned, along with the plans that had led to the demolition of so many little streets.

He glanced back once, looking at the way he had come with intense concern, as though to make certain that he had it right. It was hard to fill in the detail, what had once been walls and doors and entry gates where now there was only rubble and memory, but he felt that he had it right. That there had been no mistake and he had left the child where that first one had been found all those years ago.

His bike was parked in the shadows between two streetlamps. The chrome gleamed when it caught the light. He straddled it, holding the machine firmly between long legs, feeling in his pocket for something before kicking the bike into life. The skin of his back crawled, itching and tightening as though in preparation for what he had in mind. The faces etched into his flesh – designs in ink drawn by an artist so talented that sometimes her skills seemed like another kind of magic – moved across the surface of his back.

He paused, checking once more that the paper was still inside the pocket of his jacket, taking it out for a moment and examining the clipping in the harsh yellow light. The eyes of a child met his own.

Chapter Six

A long way from Mallingham, Katie woke to a chill grey dawn, her body stiff and cold from the night she had spent in the bus shelter. She had taken the night bus north, looking on the map and choosing something that went in approximately the right direction. The result was that she was now fifty miles from home, numb to the bone, hungry and appalled at how much it was going to cost her to get to Mallingham if her last journey was anything to judge by.

She'd have to hitch a lift. Her money wasn't going to get her anywhere near if she relied on buses, and trains were obviously out. Her mum said that they were always more expensive.

She found a small café, open for the workers on the early shift, and bought herself some breakfast. As she ate, she looked at her map again, grateful to be out of the cold and damp for at least a little while. Her best plan was to head for the motorway, she thought. She'd often seen people standing on the slip roads holding cardboard signs.

She found a stack of old boxes behind the café and took some time to make one for herself, drawing the letters large and filling them in with scribbled ballpoint pen. On the map, the M1 didn't look so far away and Leicester couldn't be more than another fifty after that.

From there she could get to Mallingham. There was bound to be another bus, it must be almost local service from there.

Armed with her sign and an ill-founded optimism borne largely from an inability to read maps, Katie set off on what would prove to be a long miserable walk.

At just before nine o'clock on the morning of the 22nd the office workers at Triton Textiles were about to start their day. Their factory had once been part of a small industrial estate, but redevelopment had left it as isolated as St Leonard's Church, which could be seen across the wasteland. It was a dog that caught their attention, one of several strays they frequently saw and often fed. This one was a black and tan and looked as though it might have had some German shepherd in its ancestry. It was circling a mound of bricks, from time to time rearing up on its hind legs and using its front paws to prod at whatever had attracted it. Then it thrust its head forward and pulled hard at something.

'Must have found a rat,' Sheila Brown commented.

'That's not a rat, it looks like . . .'

Mary Anthony did not finish her sentence. She stood quite still for a moment and then ran out of the door and down the stairs. Sheila followed her, not quite knowing what was going on but panicked by Mary's sudden urgency.

She caught up with her friend as Mary was trying to coax the dog away from whatever he'd found. 'Grab him,' she told Sheila. 'Don't worry, he won't bite.'

Sheila got hold of the dog as best she could and held him away from Mary, who was advancing on the pile of bricks, a look of horror on her face. She turned slowly to Sheila. 'Go and call the police. Now!' she shouted.

For a moment Sheila just stared at her. 'What is it? What can you see?'

'It's a child,' Mary told her. 'Oh, my God. He's dead.'

Ray had been out of the office for most of the day. When he returned, just after five, George was already there and Sarah arrived to meet him only a few minutes later. There were a dozen messages waiting on the answerphone.

'We have to get a secretary,' George said.

'Can we afford one?'

'Can't afford not to.'

Ray recalled the woman he had met when he had gone to see Martha. Rowena something or other, he thought. Martha had mentioned later in their conversation that Rowena was looking for work and had just taken a computer course. He made a mental note to phone Martha and ask about her and then mention it to George.

'What messages have I got?'

'One from Old Brothers. They liked our presentation and want a quote and some further advice on implementing the system. Couple of other enquiries coming from that advert we placed in the *Mercury* and someone called Martha wanting you. She sounded upset.'

'Martha?' He was genuinely surprised.

'Isn't that the friend you saw yesterday?' Sarah asked.

Ray nodded and reached for the phone.

Martha was at St Leonard's. 'Have you heard the news or seen the papers?' she demanded.

'No, I haven't. What's happened?'

'I've been trying to reach you all day,' she told him. 'It's about that little boy, Ian Thomason, who disappeared. He's dead. They found him near the church on the wasteground. He was under a blanket and laid out like my Roger.'

Chapter Seven

Katie had walked for miles. And hours. The motorway had been so much further than it had looked on the map. Finally, though, she had been given a lift and the middle-aged couple who picked her up seemed very nice, despite the fact that she was soaking wet and dripping all over their upholstery. They were Martyn Shaw's people, but Katie didn't know that. They did not go out of their way to advertise the fact. The woman wore a small pendant around her neck that carried the symbol of the Eyes of God – a small, stylized eye within a circle – but this was concealed beneath her shirt and Katie didn't see it.

By the time they had travelled a few miles up the motorway Katie realized she had problems. The couple seemed to know that she had run away from home despite her protestations that she was going to see friends and her parents knew all about it. She tried to lie about her age but the woman gave her a look which said she didn't buy it and the man asked, 'Why not use my mobile? Phone your Mum and Dad and at least let them know you are safe.'

As a runaway, Katie thought, she was pretty useless. But these people seem so nice, so concerned, and she knew her mum and dad would be going through hell, so in the end she agreed and called home. It was very hard trying to explain what had made her run away, especially in front of strangers. She just kept saying, 'I had to,' and 'Sorry about the money,' not knowing what else to tell them and horribly aware of how she slurred her words.

'The money doesn't matter,' her mother told her. 'Katie, please, just come home. Or let us know where you are and we'll come and get you.'

Then the woman spoke to Katie's mother and promised they would drop her off at the nearest police station when they left the motorway. She gave her mother their mobile number and their names and did her best to reassure her that Katie would be fine and home again soon. Katie wanted desperately to go along with this, but something stopped her. She pretended to agree but she had decided, first chance she got, that she'd make a run for it. The compulsion to follow the dream was just too strong.

There was, thought Ray, something almost mystical about the piece of plastic tape that separated a crime scene from the rest of the world. It was such an insubstantial barrier and yet it might have had the appearance and substance of the Berlin Wall for the effect it had. On one side of the tape life went on as it always had done. On the other life as most people knew it ceased to be and became other-worldly, sinister and terrible. Only the fear and the pain crossed the barrier, creeping out to poison any that came within range.

There was a single officer left on duty to fend off the curious, though the pouring rain was doing his job for him. Tarpaulin had been rigged over the site and he stood in the shelter, trying hard to avoid the runnels of water that flooded off the edge of it. Ray didn't recognize him and did not feel like introducing himself at that moment. Martha was crying. Sarah, who had driven him here, stood a few feet back from them both, separated by the gulf of their common experience, another border as mystical and insubstantial as the crime-scene tape.

'It's the same place,' said Martha. 'The same place and he was laid out the same way. That bastard Lee's dead and they've come to finish what he started.'

Ray wrapped an arm around her shoulders. He had left his raincoat in the car and his hair was plastered close to his head, his jacket soaked through.

'It's not the same, Martha,' he insisted. 'It can't be. I won't let it be.'

He looked across at the young officer and remembered himself eleven years before. He had been a sergeant then and this pile of rubble had been St Leonard's Vicarage and the boy lying on the front steps, covered by a rough blanket, had been Martha's son.

When they finally drove away, Ray insisted that they take a detour. He directed Sarah through what was left of the terraced back streets, ordering her to stop opposite a new supermarket and then, a little later, by another building site.

'What are we looking for?' Sarah wanted to know.

'I wanted to see the places where the other children were found,' Ray told her.

Sarah looked at him sharply. 'You think she could be right?' she asked fearfully.

Ray looked at her but said nothing.

Chapter Eight

It seemed like for ever before Katie and the couple she had hitched a ride with left the motorway. Their names were Emma and Bill and they had done their best to make her feel at ease and confide in them, asking her questions about her home and her studies and whether she had any pets. The sort of questions her friends' parents might ask when they were trying hard to be nice but really hadn't got a clue.

Katie did her best to reply in the spirit in which the enquiries were made, but she wasn't really interested, too involved with her plans for escape.

Twice after making the phone call they tried to get her to say where it was she was going and what she had planned to do when she got there. She could answer only with embarrassed silences and finally pretended to go to sleep to avoid their questions. Tired as she was from her long walk, the hardest thing was keeping this pretence from descending into the real thing and she was relieved when finally the car's deceleration and the change in the sound of tyres on the road surface alerted her to the fact that they had left the motorway.

'Where are we?' she asked, pretending to wake.

Emma glanced at her and her look told Katie once again that she had fooled no one. It occurred to her belatedly that there had been no change in the rhythm of conversation between the two when they had supposed her to be sleeping. Katie knew from experience that the first thing adults did when they thought you couldn't hear was to talk about you.

'We're just coming up to Northampton,' Emma told her. 'We told your mum and dad we'd drop you off at the police station and of course we'll stay until we know you're going to be all right.'

Katie turned away from the woman's searching gaze and huddled back into her silence in the corner of the car. Northampton, where on the map was that? She remembered seeing it and knew it was still roughly in the right direction, but she couldn't quite place it in relation to Mallingham. She thought about getting her map book from her pack and having a look, but decided against it almost at once. It might look too suspicious, and Emma, Katie felt, was suspicious enough of her already. Besides, she wanted to be ready to make a run for it as soon as the car stopped and trying to shove a map book back into her pack would just waste time. Anyway, she thought, at eight o'clock in the evening it was now far too dark to see.

She tried to pay attention to her surroundings without making it obvious. Bill seemed intent on getting her to talk again.

'Your mum and dad are going to be relieved to see you.'

'Yes.'

'They must have been worried sick.'

'Yes, I know.'

'You seem like a nice kid. It must have been pretty

serious for you to take off like that. Knowing how worried they would be.'

Katie nodded but said nothing.

'So, why d'you do it, Katie? What went wrong? You know, I'm sure if you told them they could sort it out.'

'Maybe it's something you feel might shock them?' Emma put in. 'But parents aren't that easily shocked, you know. They'd much rather be put in the picture so they can help.'

'I know,' Katie told them. 'Really, I know.'

Emma turned around as far as her seat belt would allow and scrutinized her closely. It was, thought Katie, as if she was trying to decide whether or not to tell a secret of her own. Katie's heart sank, certain that the woman was going to launch into one of those 'I remember what it was like to be a teenager' talks that adults seemed to be so fond of and always did all wrong. One thing about her mum was that she didn't do that sort of thing. She'd talk about the stuff she'd done as a kid. Laugh about it, even cry sometimes, but she never made out that she knew what Katie thought and felt just because she'd once been that age. 'It's different for everyone,' was Lisa's line. 'I'll always try to understand, baby, but never assume I do. Sometimes I need things spelling out, you know.'

Katie wished she'd been able to do that this time. Spell things out for her mum and ask for her help. It was the voices in her dreams that stopped her. That and the real fear that if her parents once knew then they would become a part of it, and the danger would reach out and encompass them too. Them and Gavin and all the family that she had ever known and cared about.

They were approaching the outskirts of Northampton now and Katie looked eagerly out of the window for some further clue. How far from Mallingham? Where should she go when she got away from these two?

She could barely hide her excitement when she saw a sign saying Leicester was only twenty miles away. Would there be a bus service? Would it run tonight? And, if it did, would she have enough cash? She thought so, but she had never travelled alone before and so far all of her suppositions had turned out to be wrong.

Watching out of the window, Katie figured that Northampton was based on a complicated one-way system that spiralled in towards the centre. Bill was trying to work out the route to the police station. They had slowed down approaching a set of red traffic lights and Katie decided that it was now or never. Once they reached the police station there'd be people who would give chase; it would no longer be just Bill and Emma. But, Katie thought, they could hardly run after her if she left them at the lights. They were third in the queue of traffic, and a line of cars stretched behind them. Once they had stopped, Katie waited, watching for the lights to turn from red to amber. She was sitting on the driver's side and a second line of traffic had pulled up alongside. The lights changed. Katie wrenched the door open and leapt out, dragging her pack behind her. The door clanged against the car next to them and she ran, leaving it wide open. The lights had turned to green and the cars in front of Bill's had moved off. She looked back long enough to see him get out of his car and the driver of the car she had slammed the door into also leaping out and shouting at Katie, then turning to yell at Bill.

Katie just ran. She could hear car horns sounding behind her and she felt a pang of guilt at having caused trouble for people who were genuinely trying to help. But the voices in her head were now screaming at her to get away.

She had to reach Mallingham.

Ray and Sarah returned briefly to the office. George was still there. He had been phoning around to find out who was heading the murder inquiry. It was a man called DI Beckett. Ray vaguely recalled him but didn't think that they had ever met. Dave Beckett was a newcomer, after his time.

Ray went back home with Sarah rather than be alone, but even with her sleeping close beside him he could not quieten his mind. In the early hours of the morning he got out of bed and went to stand by the window, gazing out across the open fields towards the city lights. Beyond that and out of sight over the horizon he could imagine the lights of Mallingham. He saw in his mind's eye the crime-scene tape stretched around the pathetic little pile of bricks and rubble on which young Ian Thomason had lain. But it was a face from an earlier time that filled his mind. Heavy lids drawn closed over dark brown eyes. Coarse, close-cropped hair dampened by morning dew and slender hands folded pathetically over a narrow chest.

A small body covered by a rough blanket. Martha's child.

Miles away, in Mallingham, Timothy Westerby could not sleep either. His dog, Ben, had been missing all afternoon and had not returned in the evening. They had telephoned the RSPCA and asked all the neighbours but no one had seen him. Timothy was heartbroken, convinced that the dog had been hit by a car or stolen.

The small sound of the back-gate latch fetched him out of bed and over to the window. A soft whimpering came up from the yard. Tim had the window open and was leaning out. The dog stared up at him and the whimpering became little yelps of pleasure.

Tim ran down the stairs and unlocked the back door. His parents would never see him alive again.

Chapter Nine

For Katie this was another bitterly cold morning. Rain mixed with snow had begun to fall and the sharp wind had risen. She had spent the night wandering around the town, keeping to the centre, where there was most light and people. She had tried hard to look as though she was going somewhere, but even so she had been propositioned twice and a group of drunken youths had shouted at her suggestively. She had done all she could to ignore this, though she had been badly frightened by it. It was so alien to the protected life she led with her family. Finally she had climbed over a gate into a park and sheltered in the bandstand. It was at least a little drier there, if still as cold, and she was tormented by worry about her parents and what they must be thinking. She had not slept.

At about six-thirty she wandered back out of the park and into the main streets. She was cold and felt dirty and unkempt; catching sight of herself in shop windows merely confirmed this. Her hair was matted and wet, and even in the poor reflection offered by the glass she could see the dark shadows beneath her eyes.

She found a McDonald's and cleaned herself up as best she could in their washroom before ordering some breakfast. With her face washed and her hair dried under the hand-dryer and then combed at least she felt a little more human, and with some food inside her she was more ready to face the day. She asked for directions to the bus station, but she was worried that the police would be looking for her. Emma and Bill had said they were taking her to the police station, so presumably they would have reported her missing and the local police would have been given a description. Katie knew she'd just have to chance it. There was no way she could walk to Leicester – her feet still hurt from her long walk of the day before. Her fashionable trainers had not proved up to the challenge and her heels were sore and her toes blistered.

Buses to Leicester ran almost every hour from nine o'clock. There was nothing direct to Mallingham, she was told, but it should be easy to get a direct bus from Leicester. Katie was still worried about being seen and she kept moving, wandering around the area, looking in shop windows and trying to seem as though she had somewhere to go and the right to be there, but she was relieved – profoundly relieved – when the bus arrived and she could get on board. She found a seat near the back, from where she could watch passengers getting on. It was close to the emergency exit. She thought that if the worst came to the worst she could at least get out that way. She was very tired and the bus was warm. She took off her jacket, pulled her backpack onto her knees for safekeeping and tugged the jacket over herself, knowing that as soon as the bus started to move she would be unable to resist going to sleep. Mallingham was at last in her sights and the man she saw in her dreams would be there. She knew it.

Chapter Ten

DI Dave Beckett had been drafted in from the local serious-crimes unit, but Mallingham was not new to him. He had served in Leicester as a sergeant, so he knew the area well. Around him the incident room was taking shape and the familiarity of it was somehow soothing. He had heard someone once say that habit was like the smooth groove in the brain and this was certainly his smooth groove. No matter how traumatic or difficult, he always found it comforting to have the same familiar setting around him. The notice-boards, the pinboards with their photographs, the organized routine of investigation and collation. It helped him get his mind into gear and his thoughts in order.

It was a measure of the seriousness of this case that he had been called in from the beginning, instead of the preliminary investigation being left to local officers. He'd been warned that feelings in Mallingham were running high and this murder, together with the latest disappearance, coming as it did on the back of Harrison Lee's death, would make liaison with the public a priority and the calming of their understandable fears a difficult task for anyone to take on. When Ian Thomason had been found, one small detail had turned this from a simple murder inquiry – if they were ever simple – into something potentially more explosive. Only one member of the public – the woman who had first found the body – had been privy to this and she had failed to see the significance, being more concerned – admirably so – in keeping the scene from being contaminated by others than on close examination of a child who was so obviously dead. Beckett reflected that sometimes television could be useful. The woman had followed television crime procedure to the letter, warding people away from the scene and keeping them at a good distance from the body. Beckett knew that she had been relieved just to have something to do, to take her mind from the enormity of what had occurred, but it had stood them in good stead. The tiny marks drawn on the boy's hands, the woman had noted but not mentioned until Beckett did, slipping it casually into the conversation as he took her statement.

'I saw something,' she said. 'My kids are always drawing on themselves. I tell them not to, but that's kids for you.'

For Beckett, and those now involved in the investigation, that little drawing was what made all the difference. The eye confined within a circle neatly and beautifully drawn in indelible ink, one in each small palm.

Someone somewhere wanted them to link this to the death of Harrison Lee. Beckett was keeping an open mind, but his superiors were deeply worried. There was just the chance that someone linked to Lee was doing this out of perverse remembrance of him. Mallingham of eleven years before had been a town paralysed by terror, its inhabitants unable to deal with the fear that the deaths of three children in nine days had caused. Those who had been on the force at the time would never forget the emotional drain, the sheer terror that every parent in the area suffered. No one wanted that again.

Beckett perched himself on the edge of his desk. He knew that the fax he held in his hand would not bring welcome news to those he had assembled for the inquiry. He had hoped that someone from the original investigation would be available to help and the obvious choice had been the person who had headed it. He might be able to bring them up to speed much faster than a simple reading of the reports. Beckett believed in personal experience, that there was no substitute for it, and that a written report only ever gave part of the story.

A dozen officers had now assembled in the incident room. These would be his key personnel. Two of them had been around eleven years before, both constables at the time. One was now a detective sergeant, the other still in uniform.

'When I spoke to you yesterday, I had hoped that the DCI Bryant as was would come on board as an adviser. And I'm afraid I've got some bad news for you.' He paused and glanced around the room. These were all experienced officers, but even experienced officers had their superstitions and this news would do nothing to help allay them. 'I'm afraid that Bryant is dead,' he said, looking around the room again and watching them process this information.

There were shock, surprise and knowing looks from one or two of them.

'So how did he die, sir?' Sergeant Emma Thorn asked him.

'Heart attack,' Beckett said. 'He died a few days ago, on the 18th as it happens, same day as Harrison Lee.'

Again the looks of shock and surprise.

'It was a family celebration apparently. They had dinner and everything was fine, then Bryant seemed to become agitated about something, said he saw someone outside in the garden. He got up, went to the window and then collapsed. They tried to revive him at the scene and the paramedics did all they could, but he was dead on arrival at hospital.'

Emma Thorn was looking at him and he knew what the next question would be.

'Who did he think he saw, sir?' she asked.

Beckett shifted uncomfortably. 'It was dark in the garden,' he said, 'but apparently Bryant thought he saw Harrison Lee.'

Chapter Eleven

The bus pulled into St Margaret's bus station at just after eleven and Katie got out into yet more rain. Wind whipped around the bus station complex, channelled down the side streets, and whistled through the automatic doors of the waiting room. She looked around for the ticket office. She felt much more positive now, despite the shock of renewed cold after the over-heated bus. She had slept for a while and felt better for it, though she was hungry again and still damp from the earlier rain she had endured.

She asked for a ticket to Mallingham and was delighted to find that a bus left in only ten minutes' time. Her joy turned to dismay, however, when she tried to find her purse. It had gone. She ran back to the Northampton bus, still parked on its stand, and the driver helped her to look, but the purse was nowhere to be seen and Katie was forced to the dreadful conclusion that it had been stolen while she slept. Close to tears, she thanked the driver for his help and got off the bus, wondering what to do next. She had no money, her feet hurt and it was bitterly cold. Rain mixed with snow and blown by the strong wind seemed to fly almost at right angles to the ground.

Katie went into the public toilets and examined her feet in one of the cubicles. Her heels had bled and the dried blood had stuck her socks firmly to the open cuts. Wincing, she pulled them away and padded both her heels and her blistered toes with toilet paper before easing her trainers back on. There was nothing for it. She had not come this far to turn back now, though she was sorely tempted to reverse the charges and call her mum and dad. The need to speak to them and get them to come and fetch her was so strong that she began to cry again. She wiped her eyes impatiently and turned up the collar of her jacket, wishing that she had a hood or even one of Gavin's stupid hats. Another look at her map told her that she wanted the Nottingham road and she set off again, no longer even really certain why she was doing this, knowing only that she had come this far and had to finish her journey now.

It was almost four o'clock before Ray returned to the office. He had been to see Martha after the news of Timothy Westerby's disappearance broke and done his best to calm her down. He had also spoken to Rowena and arranged for her to come into the office the following day. She seemed delighted at the prospect of working for them. Ray had told her all he could about what the job would entail, then left the rest to George to explain. Apart from answering telephones, he had little idea of what a secretary did, never having had need of one before.

Parking outside the office in Clarendon Park was awkward and Ray was slightly irritated to see that someone in a Ford Mondeo was in his usual spot. He parked a little way down the street and walked back, shrugging his shoulders against the damp weather. It had stopped raining but the sky was thickly grey and overcast, as if the artist who had painted it had been overly fond of impasto and lacking in subtlety. A man was standing in the Victorian tiled lobby. He was leaning against the walls and had the look of someone who'd been waiting there for quite some time. He stepped forward as Ray came through the door.

'Ray Flowers?'

'Yes.' Ray eyed the other man thoughtfully. He was police. Ray could recognize the invisible badge – he still wore it himself, even though he was now retired.

'I'm Detective Inspector Beckett,' the man said. 'Can you spare me some of your time?'

Ray nodded slowly. 'I've been expecting you,' he said. 'But I hoped you wouldn't come.' It was final confirmation of what Martha had feared.

As Katie walked she thought about the recurring dream she'd had ever since she could remember. In fact, the dream was probably the earliest thing she could remember, and so intertwined was it with real events that she was no longer certain which part was dream and which true.

She vividly recalled the explosion. A howl of noise beginning deep beneath her feet, rumbling like thunder from below the ground and spreading upwards until it engulfed her, drowning out her screams. Before that she could remember little – there were only fragmented images.

A woman bending to pick her up and holding her tightly, kissing her. Someone giving her a cup of orange and telling her to drink, and Katie protesting that she didn't like orange juice. And then, of course, the boy. He had taken the cup away from her before she finished drinking it, leading her out of the room and downstairs into the hall. She remembered the touch of his hand, how he held her so tightly and talked to her and told her that everything was going to be all right. He had seemed so big, almost grown-up, but in retrospect she realized that he was probably only thirteen or so, just much bigger than she was.

He had taken her down through the hall, into the kitchen and beyond that into a long cupboard that ran beneath a staircase. The door to the cupboard was small and cut at a funny angle at the top. The boy opened it and told her to get inside. He made it sound like a game. Katie remembered that she had felt so sleepy and that the boy had kept talking to her, telling her not to go to sleep, that she must try to stay awake. He had coaxed her into the cupboard, making a nest of cushions for her to sit in. The cushions he must have taken from sofas earlier, as she recognized the pattern. And then he disappeared for a little while, coming back with a long rug that had been in the hall. He folded it several times and then put it into the hole in front of Katie so that it was between her and the door. She could just see over it if she stood on tiptoe, but it made the cupboard very dark.

'I'm scared,' Katie had said.

The boy put his finger to his lips and shushed her. 'It's all right,' he said. 'We are playing hide-and-seek. You want to hide, don't you?'

Katie remembered that she nodded. She was so sleepy now that it was too much trouble to argue. And still the boy kept talking to her, telling her not to fall asleep.

'This is too dark,' Katie had complained again as he began to close the door. She didn't remember being scared, just very tired.

'I'll leave the door open a little bit if you promise to be quiet,' he said. 'But you must promise to be really, really quiet.'

Katie did not understand why but she nodded sleepily and lay down in the nest of cushions. She remembered the little shaft of light entering through the partly open door. It had looked pretty against the darkness. She seemed to remember the boy hesitating, but that might have been a part of her dream, she didn't know. The door closed then, but she must have fallen asleep soon after, because she didn't cry and she wasn't scared any more. The next thing was the explosion, the enormity of sound that echoed around the tiny cupboard and still filled her dreams all these years after.

It was a relief, thought Dave Beckett, to be talking to someone who had been there before and had an idea of what to expect. Briefly he outlined the incidents so far, telling Ray how the boy had been found and about the drawings on his hands. Ray said little. He sat cradling a mug of hot tea, listening intently.

'Eye within a circle,' he said finally. 'It's strange, you know, that the cult still uses the same symbol. I'd have thought they would want a change after all the lousy publicity it must have brought them.'

Beckett shrugged. 'I don't know anything about that,' he said. 'I have little time for religion of any kind.'

He took a sip of his tea. It was still extremely hot, but very welcome. He leaned back in his chair and regarded Flowers thoughtfully, taking in the scarred face and hands and the lopsided smile as Ray grinned at him, acknowledging his scrutiny and returning it. Beckett had warm brown eyes and greying hair, complete with a distinctive widow's peak. He was, guessed Ray, middle forties, somewhere close to his own age.

'Look a bit odd, don't I?' he commented.

Beckett shrugged again. 'The child that they rescued that night. The one they called Katie.'

'I remember her,' Ray said. 'A tiny little blonde thing dressed in a Bugs Bunny night-shirt. Not a mark on her. At the time it seemed almost miraculous.'

'She ran away from her foster home two days ago,' Beckett told him. 'Her foster parents think she might be headed this way. They had a phone call from a couple who picked her up on the motorway. They were going to hand her over to the police in Northampton, but she gave them the slip. They called Katie's parents to let them know, but we've heard nothing from them since.'

Ray frowned. 'You know for sure that she got away from them?' he asked,

Beckett smiled. 'Oh, yes,' he said. 'They stopped at red lights and she waited until they changed, then flung the door open and ran off. The car door hit another car in the next lane and the driver demanded they do something about it. It barely marked the paintwork but he was not in the mood to put up with any of it.'

'So presumably you can trace them through their insurance details?' Ray said.

'If it were that easy,' Beckett replied. 'The driver that she hitched the lift from, he calls himself Bill Wyatt, he bunged the man some cash and drove away. The driver of the other car was annoyed enough to report it, but we've no idea who this Bill and the woman, Emily or Emma as she called herself, could be. Might be they just didn't want to get any more involved. Might be something more. We have a mobile phone number for them, from when they phoned Katie's parents. But the number seems to be unavailable, as they say. The phone's certainly not been switched on since.'

Ray sat for a moment thinking about this. 'What makes them think she wanted to come to Mallingham?' he said. 'What made her run away? Are we sure it's connected?'

Beckett nodded slowly. 'Her parents say that she was having nightmares. She dreamed that someone was coming back, but she couldn't say who. Her mum told us that Katie was scared. Really scared. But she didn't seem able to explain herself. Apparently she's barely spoken since the explosion. She does OK at school, writing and such, and has her friends, but she still has problems with talking to people, especially if it's connected with that night.'

'Someone coming back,' Ray mused thoughtfully. 'Do you think she meant Harrison Lee?'

Beckett shook his head. 'I don't know,' he said. 'I hoped you might be able to tell me.'

Chapter Twelve

By the time Katie eventually stumbled into Mallingham she looked a wreck and she knew it. Drowned rat did not even begin to describe her. She asked for directions twice before she managed to find the police station. Both times people shied away from her as though they feared contamination.

Katie had had enough. She was tired, hungry, soaking wet and very miserable, and she had made up her mind. She would go to the police station, ask to see someone in charge, explain what she had come for and then let them send her home. As far as she was concerned, she'd done what she had felt compelled to do. Now she just wanted to go home.

She walked up to the front desk of the station. The vinyl tiles had been newly washed and Katie spread muddy footprints and fat drops of dirty rainwater all over the clean surface. She looked down guiltily at her feet and then up at the desk sergeant, who was glowering at her.

'I'm sorry,' she said hesitantly. Then, 'I think you might be looking for me.' She certainly hoped they were.

The man gave her a funny look and then beckoned her closer. Katie gave one last despairing glance at her feet and the mess she was creating and walked forward. She was shaking with cold now, shivering uncontrollably, soaked right through to her underwear by the torrential rain.

'And who might you be?' the desk sergeant asked her. 'And why might we be looking for you?'

'My name is Katie,' she said, 'Katie Fellows, and I ran away from home.'

She looked so pathetic, no one could have failed to take pity on her. The desk sergeant was no exception. He had not long started his shift and he remembered the name Katie Fellows from a note in the day-book. Beckett wanted to talk to her if she turned up, though no one had really thought she would. He called for a WPC and had her find spare clothes, a blanket and a cup of tea, and half an hour later Katie, her hair still wet but feeling somewhat warmer in her borrowed clothes, was sitting in an interview room with Sergeant Emma Thorn, waiting for a call to be put through to her foster parents.

'Your mum said you were having bad dreams,' Emma Thorn said. 'That seems like a funny reason for running away from home.'

Katie nodded. 'I know it is.' She swallowed nervously, wondering where to begin. 'It's him,' she said finally. 'He wants to finish things.' She shook her head, puzzled as to how to go on, how to explain to this young policewoman. Emma, the second Emma she had met in as many days, but different. She looked confident and calm and didn't direct at her any of those 'I know what it's like to be a teenager' glances.

Emma Thorn looked Katie straight in the eye as though genuinely curious and said, 'Can you tell me about your dreams?' She waited a moment and then went on, 'Or would you rather wait until your mum's here? I mean, you don't even know me, do you?'

Katie sighed. She closed her eyes and wrapped both hands around the mug of tea. She had never felt so tired or so completely ridiculous. All that effort to run away and now she'd handed herself in at the local police station in Mallingham and was likely to be sent home without finding the man who could help her, without achieving any of the things that she'd set out to do. It would have helped, thought Katie, if she had known what those things were to start with.

Emma Thorn reached across the table and touched her hand. 'It's OK,' she said. 'At least *you're* safe, that's the main thing.'

Katie opened her eyes and looked at her. Something in the way the woman had spoken told Katie that she wasn't the only person on Emma's mind. 'Who isn't safe?' she asked. 'Who has he taken this time?'

Since that day he had blocked out the sun, keeping his curtains closed and opening his windows to the world only at night. And he had learned as he grew older to re-create the images, the falling angels reaching out their hands towards the earth, and where once he had to be content with the wings of moths he could now breathe life into his own images. Brush and pigment obeyed his hand, bringing his vision to life as the first artist had done all those years before. Pigments oxidized with blood to give them power, and the wings of his beloved moths had been collected up and stowed away beneath the altar.

And now the old one was dead and had sent out his soul, and the chosen one was ready to be reborn.

Chapter Thirteen

DI Dave Beckett was called at five with the news that Katie had turned up at Mallingham. He had been on his way home, but he swung the car round at the next roundabout and headed back for the police station. His afternoon had been productive, Ray had been eager to help in any way he could, though some of his ideas were a little bizarre, to say the least. He seemed to have been drawn into the thoughts and feelings of the Eyes of God in a way that Beckett himself didn't think he would ever have allowed. That said, Ray's record as a police officer was excellent and his recent involvement in exposing high-level police corruption in the wake of one of the biggest drug busts the area had ever seen was to be applauded, though Beckett was not naïve enough to think that everyone would see it that way. Ray's investigation had implicated several senior officers, seriously damaging public confidence.

It had been Emma Thorn who had called to give him the news. Katie had apparently spoken to her foster parents and they were on their way to Mallingham.

'She's deeply disturbed about something,' Emma Thorn had said.

'Has she explained why she came here?'

'She talks about a dream. She knew that something bad had happened, that someone would die. She's quite convinced that Harrison Lee isn't dead. At least I think that's what she means, it's not easy to be sure. I got her to write things down for me in the end, she seemed to find that easier to deal with than having to tell me out loud.'

'And what do you make of her?' Beckett asked.

Emma paused before answering, then she said, 'I like her. I think she's a decent kid. But something really deep is troubling her and won't give her any peace. I don't even think she knows why she's here.'

Beckett promised to get there as soon as he could, but he knew he'd be caught in the tail-end of the rush-hour traffic and it might take some time.

He'd been using the hands-free set to talk to Emma, but he realized to his annoyance that Ray's number had not yet been programmed into his phone. He found a bus stop and pulled over before dialling Ray's number. He was not sure why he felt compelled to do this, but he did. He justified it by telling himself that Ray had been concerned for Katie and had also been present the night she was found in the aftermath of the explosion. An encounter between them might trigger something in the girl's mind.

Ray picked up on the second ring. If he was surprised to hear from Beckett again so soon, he didn't say so.

'I'll be there as soon as I can,' he promised. 'Thank God she's safe.'

Beckett rang off. He echoed those sentiments. He just wished he could feel confident about Tim Westerby's chances.

Ray had told him something useful that afternoon,

something he had been unaware of. The location of this latest murder had a clear connection with the past. Roger Joyce's body had been found in the same place, which Ray reckoned had been a vicarage. Ray considered it was likely that if Tim Westerby was dead, his body would be found in the same place as that of the second child eleven years ago. Phillip Abrahams had been left close to an old cinema. It had already been closed back then, but now, Ray thought, it was the site of a new supermarket.

'It's a long time ago,' he'd told Beckett. 'I'm not dead sure of the location, there's been so much redevelopment in Mallingham, but you could look it up. It wouldn't be so hard to find out exactly.'

Beckett had put two officers on the problem, knowing that it meant sifting through old files and would take time. And he didn't think Tim Westerby had much time left.

Beckett's first impression of Katie was of an exhausted child who just wanted to go to sleep. An appropriate adult had been summoned in the shape of a social worker who had clearly been doing her best to ingratiate herself with Katie and was getting nowhere fast. Emma Thorn had taken her down to the canteen and fed her, and that had been the most positive move, Beckett thought, that anyone had made so far. She certainly seemed to prefer Emma to the social worker who had been assigned to look after her, greeting her with a tired smile when she came into the room with Beckett.

'This is DI Dave Beckett,' Emma Thorn told Katie. 'If you're really good you might get to call him Dave.'

Katie gave her another smile, but it was clear that she was losing interest.

Dave Beckett sat down at the table opposite. 'Have they sorted out where you're staying for the night?' he asked.

She nodded. 'Mum and Dad are coming.'

Beckett looked across at Emma for confirmation. 'No more than a couple of hours up the motorway,' she said. 'We thought it might be best for Katie to hang on here until her parents arrived and then they can all go to the hotel together.'

Beckett nodded. She was a pretty kid, he thought. Round face with hair that had been cut into a neat bob, though two days of neglect and soaking weather had left it looking far from its best. The sweater she had been loaned was several sizes too big and the sleeves came down over her hands. She looked very young and very vulnerable, the oversized clothes just adding to the impression of fragility she seemed to convey.

'You came here looking for someone?' Beckett asked.

Katie nodded.

'So, do you know his name?'

She shook her head.

'And when you do find him,' Beckett asked her, 'what do you want him to do?'

'Stop it all from happening again. Make the other one go away.'

For a moment Beckett regarded her thoughtfully,

questions clamouring in his head. Then suddenly Katie looked towards the door. Her whole body stiffened and she got excitedly to her feet.

'He's here,' she said.

At that moment the door opened and a constable came to tell Beckett that Ray Flowers had arrived.

Chapter Fourteen

George got up early on the morning of 24 February. He was naturally an early riser, not liking to waste what he saw as the best part of the day, and this morning he had a special task in mind. He had begun to pack up his home in preparation for moving and planned to put much of the furniture in store until such time as he found somewhere suitable. Until then he had rented a flat close to the office.

This morning, though, he was determined to deal with the most difficult room. Jan's room. It was a task he had been putting off for a long time and the room was much as his daughter had left it. George saw no contradiction in the fact that Jan had left home a good year before she had died, that this was not a place she counted as hers any longer. To George, Jan's room was just that, hers, and would always be. Many of her things – childhood toys, favourite clothes, objects reclaimed from the flat she had shared with friends – were still there.

He had never recovered from his daughter's death. He acknowledged that freely. Jan had died of a drug overdose, the circumstances had been suspicious, as his daughter had not been a known user, and Ray had been the investigating officer. George had done everything he could to keep the case alive long after all leads had burned out and the investigating officers had been assigned elsewhere.

He had pestered Ray for weeks afterwards, calling him at work and on his private line, and he now blessed the fact that Ray had not once shown anger or resentment, even when George had been at his most aggressive and unreasonable.

A verdict of accidental death had been recorded, though George had never believed that, despite, much to his chagrin, never even coming close to proving otherwise. It had been the one time in his life when strings pulled, contacts made, favours called in had meant nothing. He had been totally helpless in the face of his own personal tragedy and he still remained unreconciled to the fact.

He had been standing in the doorway for at least fifteen minutes, unable to cross the threshold, and in the end closed the door again and went back downstairs. He had a lady who came in to clean for him three times a week. He would ask her to do it for him. Lili would understand, she knew how he felt about Jan's room.

Thinking of Jan led him back to thinking about Mitch. He had always liked her, admiring her spirit and independence, the exact qualities her father found so hard to deal with. The exact qualities he had found so hard to deal with in his own child. Patrick had called him the night before. George had not arrived home until very late and Patrick was clearly drunk. He didn't like George's answers to his questions, didn't like the fact that George had found nothing so far to support Patrick's insistence that Mitch should leave the Eyes of God.

George had watched a video of the Prophet several times since he had seen the tape at Patrick's home. He had examined the figure closely, studying Martyn Shaw as he had studied many men in his professional career. The man was sincere as far as he could see. George may not be on his wavelength as far as beliefs were concerned, but somehow he did not doubt the man's integrity. Martyn Shaw believed that he was chosen, that he had a message and it was his duty to pass it on to the world.

George could understand Mitch wanting to belong to something like this, and he wondered if her choice was so different from his own. He had been a career soldier, followed by a career in more covert activities. Membership, in effect, of a club quite as exclusive as the Eyes of God. As ready to turn away those eager but unsuitable. And this sense of belonging had been hardest to leave behind when he had quit his job. It had been more than a job, it had been a life, a total existence. In his heart of hearts he had been deeply relieved when Dignan offered him work, because it meant keeping the contact that George had most feared losing. He knew that Ray understood this, though they never discussed it. Ray was not someone who needed to belong in the same way. He made his life as a professional outsider, belonging, therefore, to a club just as exclusive as anything George could aspire to.

He thought about Patrick and wondered how he was going to cope when Mitch refused once again to come home. George knew he would have to support her decision. He knew, too, that he and Patrick were cut from the same cloth: same background, same aspirations, part of something that both their daughters had rejected, though Mitch much more positively than Jan ever had.

George sighed and wondered what really happened to the dinosaurs.

In a shocking twist of fate, Tim Westerby's body was found by children who had known him. They were walking to school in a group as usual, though today they had a couple of older brothers in tow just to make sure that they arrived safely. Children from Tim Westerby's street, who attended the same school, who played with him at break-time and argued over who should sit where at lunch.

They were a little subdued this morning, but kids, being kids, and full of restless energy, two of them had run on ahead. The old Fosse Cinema had been demolished more than a year before and a new supermarket built on the site. Now the buildings around this were coming down, what had been an ancient, run-down garage at the side of the cinema and a pub that had been closed for as long as the boys could remember. The buildings had been cordoned off and half demolished, but every day they ran to the iron railings and peered down into now empty basements where beer barrels had once been kept or, a little further along, the inspection pit in the garage where cars had been brought for repair.

They were fascinated by the exposure of the skeletons within the buildings, the reinforcing from the concrete and the invisible structure that had formerly held it all in place now laid bare. Sometimes, if they were alone, without older brothers in tow, they sneaked through the railings and prowled the site before the day's work began.

The boys knew it intimately. The difference today was that Tim was not with them.

The barking of a dog drew their attention and about twenty feet from the road, tied to a concrete reinforcing bar by a length of rope, was a springer spaniel. Both boys recognized him at once.

'That's Ben. That's Tim's dog.'

The more cautious of the two turned and shouted to his brother to come and look. The second had pushed his way through the gap in the fence and was running across the site towards the frantic animal, whose barks had become louder and more plaintive as he saw someone he recognized.

By the time the rest of the group arrived, the boy was standing beside the dog, staring down at something.

Tim Westerby lay gazing at the sky, covered to the chin by a grey blanket edged in blue. This time his hands were not crossed over his chest, as Ian Thomason's had been, but were extended to the side, palms open, and on each palm the symbol of an eye within a circle drawn clear and large.

Beckett had gone to the hotel to speak with Katie again, this time in the presence of her foster parents. Ray had joined them.

The previous night Katie had been too tired and, after Ray's arrival, too emotional to be of much use to him, but Beckett hoped that this morning things would be better. She certainly looked more rested and relaxed, sitting with her parents and brother in the hotel lounge and carrying on what looked to be a very loud conversation in sign.

Ray arrived just behind him and they went in together.

'You look much better this morning,' Ray commented.

She nodded. 'Thank you.'

Her parents rose to greet the newcomers. They still looked tense and pained, and Beckett knew they would be eager to get home. The night before, they had established that Ray was the man Katie had come to find but little more.

'What happened to your face?' she had asked him.

'What happened to your hair? Last time I saw you it reached right down your back.'

'Cut it off,' Katie told him.

'Why me?'

She shrugged. 'I saw your face. In my dream.'

'Are you sure? I can't believe that you remembered me that well. We only met that one time.'

'I know.' Katie hesitated, trying hard to get the words out without them slurring. Trying to do the things her speech therapist had told her and shaping her lips and tongue to make the sounds first. 'But you stayed with me in the ambulance,' she said. 'I sat on your knee. You sang nursery rhymes and you got them wrong.'

Ray nodded. 'I wouldn't say I actually sang them,' he said. 'But it kept you amused.'

Beckett had been listening intently. 'Why did you come here, Katie? What did you think Ray could do?'

'You said someone was coming back,' Ray said. 'Did

you mean Harrison Lee? If so, sweetheart, I can assure
you that he's dead and gone.'

Katie shook her head. 'I believe you that he's dead,'
she said. 'But he isn't gone.' She frowned, clearly trying
to root out memories that were buried very deep. 'It's
why everyone died,' she said.

'Lee was arrested. Morgan and the others would
probably have been implicated. They killed themselves.'

Katie shook her head. 'No. Morgan told them to. It
needed fire. Fire . . .' She hesitated again, trying to get it
right. 'Fire makes things clean.'

'Makes things clean? I don't understand,' Ray said.
'You mean the people who died, it was important that
they were burned? Cremated?'

Katie shook her head again. 'Not like dead people,'
she said. 'That wouldn't make it right. I heard him
talking.'

Ray waited, allowing the implications of this to sink
in, then he turned to Katie's parents. 'Have you talked to
her much about the Eyes of God?' he asked.

Guy Fellows looked uncomfortable. 'We decided that
we wouldn't bring it up,' he said, 'but that if Katie asked
questions we'd do our best to answer them. From time to
time articles have appeared in the news and we've not
discouraged her from reading them.'

Ray nodded, but anything he might have asked next
was interrupted by the ringing of a mobile.

Beckett excused himself and moved away, but his
expression as he listened to the caller told them the news.
'They've found the boy,' he said softly. 'Ray, I think you
should come with me.'

Katie stared at Ray.

'How many?' she demanded. 'How many dead?'

'Two,' Ray told her reluctantly. 'The first was taken the night Lee died.'

Katie's eyes widened and she looked at him without comment. He patted her gently on the shoulder and promised to come back.

'Well,' Beckett demanded as they left, 'what is it you both know and I don't?'

'Two deaths,' Ray said. 'We're waiting for a third. Just like last time.'

A crowd had gathered. Parents mostly from the streets that backed onto the building site. The boys who had found the body had been shepherded away, taken home by Emma Thorn, who was, with the help of a WPC, dealing with their statements.

The area had been cordoned off and the body concealed within an incident tent. Ray and Dave Beckett passed through the cordon and surveyed the scene, the semi-derelict buildings and the heavy machinery ready to finish the job. It was very close to where Ray had predicted they would find the second body.

'There, where the supermarket is now, that was the Fosse Cinema. I used to go to the pictures there. The kids' club on a Saturday.'

'You grew up round here?'

Ray nodded. 'Never much one for travelling.'

They crossed the rubble-strewn site, ducked into the shelter covering the body and stood watching as the photographer finished her job before crouching gingerly beside the corpse.

The child lay on his back and his eyes were open. Ray resisted the impulse to close them and instead avoided looking at the boy's face. He had been covered with a blanket like the last time and, as before, the blanket had been tucked around the body as though to keep him warm.

The hands were open, arms stretched out to the side, and something about the pose struck a chord with Ray, though for the moment he could not place the fleeting memory. The drawings on the hands had been made in black ink. They had been carefully inscribed, as though the design had to be exact and perfect.

A young officer pushed his way through the opening in the tent wall to tell them that SOCO had arrived. He turned white when he saw the child.

'If you're going to puke,' Ray told him sharply, 'get outside. No one pukes on my crime scene.'

The young man pulled himself upright and exited rapidly.

'*Your* crime scene?' Beckett enquired.

'Sorry. Force of habit. Probationer, is he?' He jerked his head towards the young man who had just left.

'I believe so.' Beckett gestured towards the child's hands. 'They wanted to be certain it was seen this time,' he said.

Ray nodded.

'You're serious about there being a third death, aren't you? You think the killer will take it that far.'

'I do. But I'm buggered if I know what we can do

about it. This child was taken from his own home. The first from practically outside his own front door. It's going to be no good just telling parents to keep their kids inside, and we're going to have a panic on our hands no matter what.'

'So, how do we narrow the odds?'

Ray shook his head. 'It'll be a boy,' he said. 'If he keeps to the same MO. About the same age and most likely not looking anything like the first two, so our usual cues according to type are not much help. Last time we couldn't sort out the pattern. I don't hold out much hope of this time being any different.'

'You think he could already have the third child? There was a schedule last time.'

Ray nodded. 'A rough one. And he seems to be keeping to it. My guess is that he'll take the boy tonight. Early tomorrow. Certainly before dawn.'

'Doesn't give us much to go on. You think the girl knows more than she's letting on?'

'Not consciously, no. No, I don't. She was four, five years old last time. We don't know if she met Harrison Lee or how involved she was. There were no records about her parents. We don't even know if they were there. Now we could use DNA, but that's not much help at the present.'

He sighed. 'Look, there's a chapter of the Eyes of God out Oakham way and I've got a friend who can arrange an introduction. I'll go out there and see if they can shed any light, but I'll need your sanction to tell them everything.'

Beckett nodded. 'It'll be in the evening papers anyway. We can't keep the lid on this time, there are far too many witnesses. How long will it take you? I want to schedule another talk with Katie this afternoon and I'd like you there.' He paused, a thought striking him. 'You don't think . . .'

'No, I don't. Katie was still at home the night Lee died and Ian was kidnapped. No, something triggered her desire to come here, and I'd love to know what, but I don't think she's any less of a victim than she ever was.'

'Crackpot fucking cults!' Beckett exploded.

'If only it was as simple as that,' Ray said.

Chapter Fifteen

It took some organizing. Ray called George, who then had to speak to Mitch, but within the hour Ray was on his way to Sommers House.

It was a long time since he'd had any dealings with the Eyes of God and it was not something he talked much about. He'd barely mentioned even to George just how deep his involvement had been or how much he had learned about them. George knew that he had worked on the Harrison Lee case, but not that he had once come face to face with Lee himself, that he had met Morgan and that he had, for a while, kept in contact with the relatives of those believed dead in the explosion.

Ray could not have explained what made him so cagey about discussing this time in his life, but he still found it hard. He had been one of the first officers on the scene the night that the chapterhouse exploded and had been present when Katie was found, as well as the old man who had briefly survived the explosion, only to bleed to death while they tried to free him from the wreckage.

Ray had seen something happen that night that he still could not explain. The old man had refused to give his name. He had said that names were just so much baggage and only relevant for the short time you owned them anyway. He had been so utterly unafraid that Ray had been convinced that the pain must have driven him half out of his mind.

Except that there had been no pain. Shock, the paramedics said, sometimes it did strange things to the mind. But Ray knew that they had merely been looking for explanations that their own logic and training could handle. The man had been not just free of pain; he had reached a state that Ray could describe only as ecstatic. Calm and joyful as though what he was approaching was something wonderful. He had seen the doubt in Ray's eyes and spoken to him as though he could read his thoughts.

'The greatest of adventures,' he whispered. 'Who would want to turn away?'

Ray had since read reports in the media of those who had chosen to die, believing that they were escaping this life for something far more wondrous. Those who had been part of the Heaven's Gate cult had reminded him forcibly of this old man when he had seen images from the press release that they had left behind and extracts from the video they made just before they died. That had been the closest he had come to witnessing anything like that man's certainty and unfettered joy.

When they lifted the beam from his legs, they knew that it might kill him, but they had been left with no choice. He would die anyway. They were unable to put blood into his body faster than it flowed out from his wounds. Ray had been horrified, watching the last vestiges of life ebb away from the old man's body and the spark go from his eyes, but the man had merely smiled up at him, his eyes locked on Ray's face. And then he had reached out his arms as though to embrace the air.

'Don't you feel it?' he had whispered and Ray had felt a soft wind on his face, like the passage of wings.

Sommers House glowered out of the leaden sky, the February day not kind to its limestone walls or the mossy slate of its high-pitched roof. The woods beyond enclosed the house and grounds, protecting them from the world outside.

The door opened as Ray parked the car at the end of the drive and a man came down the steps to greet him. He was about fifty years old, with faded brown hair and gentle eyes. This must be Bryn, Ray guessed, recalling George's description of him. He looked anxious, the summer-blue eyes pained and sad.

'Mr Flowers? I'm Bryn Jones. I wish I could say that you're welcome.'

He extended a hand to shake Ray's, more from courtesy, Ray felt, than any kind of pleasure.

'I'm sorry to trouble you with this,' Ray told him. 'But two boys have died already and if there's any chance you might be able to prevent a third . . .'

He left it at that. Bryn nodded and gestured for him to come inside. 'This opens too many old wounds,' he said softly. 'But from what George has told us, you already know about that.'

They were about to have lunch, having waited for him, which Ray appreciated though he was not certain about vegetarian food. There were a dozen of them gathered in the large dining room, excluding several children who had already begun to eat and indeed were almost ready to leave the table by the time he arrived.

Bryn introduced him. 'This is Mitch. My wife, Irene. Tom, who's one of our garden designers – he's getting quite a reputation locally. Amy and Ted . . .' He broke off. 'Let's just eat, shall we? And you can tell us how we can help, though I have to tell you, Ray, very few of us were around the last time. Only myself and Irene, and we weren't local, though of course we knew Morgan. The group was quite small then. And Amy too. She knew Morgan.'

Ray glanced at the woman, who raised her glass in wry response. 'Guilty,' she said. 'Though I don't know what I can tell you.'

Irene had begun to serve the meal and the children were asking to be excused. Irene waited until they were gone, their voices echoing from the playroom across the hall, before she said, 'This will mean more trouble for us, won't it?'

Ray nodded. 'I should close your gates,' he said, 'and keep them closed. The news will have broken now and by the time the evening papers come out there won't be a newspaper or TV company in the country not camping on your doorstep.'

'And there's nothing we can do about it?'

'Issue a statement perhaps, saying that you deplore what's happening and distance yourselves totally from it. Other than that, say nothing, close your gates and be prepared to ride it out.'

'For how long?'

Ray shook his head. 'That I can't tell you. Until whoever's doing this is caught. Until we put him away like we did Lee. I'm sorry. There's nothing more I can say.'

Irene nodded slowly. 'We thought we could find peace here,' she said. 'And we have. We run our courses, we live our own lives and we do no harm.'

'Someone is doing harm,' Ray told her gently. 'And in your name. I need to know anything that might help.'

'But we know nothing,' Mitch argued. 'We didn't even know about the second child or that . . . that the symbol had been drawn on his hands until George called us. We'll do anything we can, but I really don't see . . .'

'Why did Lee kill those boys?' Ray asked. 'He never explained himself, not to us, not to anyone on the outside.'

'I don't think . . .' Bryn began.

'Oh, don't give me that!' Ray sighed, aware that he was being unnecessarily sharp. 'Look, you can see the pattern as clearly as the next man. It doesn't take a genius and it doesn't even take someone with prior knowledge. Whoever's doing this is making it as obvious as they can that this is linked to what Lee had planned eleven years ago. I need to know what it was.'

Irene was poking at her food. 'What makes you think that Lee explained?' she said. 'Anyone who might have known is dead. You were there, at the chapterhouse. You saw what happened.'

'And we still don't know who died. Look, the child who survived that night – we called her Katie – she turned up in Mallingham looking for me. She's quite convinced that something even more terrible is going to happen and seems to think that I can stop it in some way. I don't know if there's anything in what she believes, but I do know that when Lee died something was set in motion and we have to stop it now before another child dies.' He paused, listening to the laughter of the children in the other room. 'It could be anyone's child,' he went on slowly. 'The second little boy was taken from his own home. The first was within yards of his front door. Can you imagine what it must be like for the parents? If one of yours was taken. Suddenly gone and you didn't know where or how. You just knew that whoever had taken them was a killer who had already taken two lives – two lives that we know about. You imagine a child of yours, scared and alone, kept God knows where and in God knows what conditions . . .'

'You've made your point!' Irene spoke sharply, then sighed. 'I know what you're saying to me. You don't need to spell it out. The fact is, we don't know what Harry Lee was planning. He was a strange man, secretive. Sometimes what he believed didn't go with what the Prophets taught. He had obsessions that even Morgan couldn't countenance and Morgan could be extreme.'

'Like what?' Ray asked.

'How much do you know about us?' Bryn asked. 'About what we believe?'

Ray considered. 'I know that you believe in something called Conservation of Matter. That you believe every atom in existence has been present in the universe since the beginning of, well, of everything. That each time some-

thing new is made – a new person, a new plant or animal
– the atomic structure will contain atoms reused, recycled
if you like, and that past life memories and so on may be a
result of this. I know that you believe in the messages of
your dreams and that you share the dream experiences.
That you believe the Earth might have been seeded from
elsewhere, either deliberately or by accident, but I don't
know why you think that.'

'Panspermia,' Amy said. It was the first time she had
spoken since Ray had sat down. 'It's becoming almost
respectable now. People like Sir Geoffrey Hoyle are talking
about it as a possibility. Did you know, for instance, that
about 70 per cent of the Earth's water had an extraterres-
trial origin and there's evidence of bacteria at least arriving
with it?'

Ray shook his head. 'I didn't know that,' he said. 'But
how does it fit with Lee?'

'Lee was a would-be alchemist,' Amy said. 'He
believed in transmutation. We all do, it's part of our
religion: that the soul, the essence of life, can be trans-
muted and purified through meditation and living a good
life. Through experience. Lee thought you could push the
process faster. Like base metals into gold. Humankind
into something else.'

'And this transmutation,' Ray asked. 'I mean, as part
of your belief system, what are you hoping to achieve by
it?'

Amy hesitated before saying, 'All religions that have a
creation myth talk about man being created in some kind
of godly image. Or man aspiring to be closer to the gods. I
suppose you could say that's what we're trying to do.

Build a society that we believe is closer to that our makers wished us to be part of. I suppose, like the Mormons believe that they can bring their ancestors into the church by baptizing them in the present, we believe that when we die we cast our souls out into the world to be reborn. To touch the souls of the unborn and maybe make a difference to what they will become. When Lee died, he would have . . .'

'Amy, this isn't for general consumption,' Bryn said. 'It's a sacred thing.'

'Murder kind of changes circumstances, Bryn. I'm sure the Prophet would want us to explain . . .' She sighed. 'If Lee sent his soul, if he didn't do as we teach . . . I'm not conveying this very well.' She looked at Ray, obviously expecting him to make fun of her.

'I just need to know,' he said. 'I'm not about to ridicule.'

'OK. Look, we believe that when we die and we send out our soul, then we have a duty to touch as many new lives as we can. We try to bless the unborn, but we have no right to, well, interfere, if you like. Individuality is such a remarkable, miraculous thing that we see it as practically sacred. Lee believed that he could send his soul out to a particular individual and that his soul could . . . kind of bond.'

'Like possession?' Ray asked.

'Possession implies unwillingness,' Bryn said softly. 'The one Lee chose, the one he sent his soul into, would have been waiting a long time to welcome him.'

*

When Ray left Sommers House he felt deeply depressed. Looking back through his rear-view, he saw Bryn closing the twin iron gates and locking them, hoping that the decorative twists of metal could keep the world at bay.

They had spoken for a little longer, but all in all Ray felt that it had been a wasted journey. He had learned a little more about Harrison Lee and they had told him about the splinter group that had broken away from the Eyes of God when Morgan had died in the explosion at the chapterhouse. Bryn and Irene claimed to have no dealings with this other group, though Ray wondered about that. It would surely have been natural to want to contact old friends even if they had gone their separate philosophical ways. The leader of this other group was a man called Edwin Farrant and Ray had made a note to himself to let Beckett know about them.

He drove back to Mallingham and went straight to the hotel. Katie and her parents were waiting for him.

'Katie wants to tell you about something,' her mother said. 'We've spent a lot of time talking about it and trying to sort out what she actually remembers from what she thinks she remembers. It might be important.'

Ray sat down and reached out for Katie's hand.

'There was a boy,' Katie told him. 'I dreamed about him. But he's real.'

'A boy? At the house?'

Katie nodded. 'He wasn't one of the ones who died,' she said. 'This was after. The night it all happened.'

'And you've never talked about him before?'

Katie shook her head. 'This boy, he told me not to drink the juice they gave me. He took the cup away and when I felt sleepy he told me that I had to stay awake. He took me down the stairs. There was a cupboard.'

She looked at Ray for confirmation. He nodded. The house had been old and large enough to have had back stairs leading from the kitchen to what had been servants' quarters.

'He put me in the cupboard. He'd put cushions in there for me to sit on. He got the rug from the hall and folded it up so that it blocked the door. He said that I had to be really quiet and not go to sleep.'

Tears had started to form at the corners of her eyes and, Ray realized, she was looking scared now, not just tired or subdued.

'He's back,' she said, 'and he wants me. He wants the three boys and then me.'

'Who wants you, Katie? And why? Do you know that?'

Katie nodded, tears coursing down her cheeks. 'Like last time,' she whispered. 'He wants to do it again.'

'How do you know any of this, Katie?' Lisa Fellows asked. 'You can't be certain the dead boys have anything to do with you. You've had no contact with any of those people, not since you were five years old.'

'I just know,' Katie protested. 'Someone put it into my head.'

Her mother looked at her in complete bewilderment and Ray knew as he left a little later that he was the only one who believed her.

Chapter Sixteen

Ray arrived at the office to find that they had acquired a new secretary.

'Oh, my God,' he said. 'Rowena. I'd forgotten all about her.'

'Fortunately, she had the sense to call first and leave her number,' George said. 'Apparently you'd been a little vague about both the job and when she should come for an interview. I called her back and she starts tomorrow.'

Ray was hungry. They ordered a take-away from an Indian restaurant on the Welford road and ate it in the tiny kitchen while Ray filled him in on the day's events.

'This second group,' George asked, 'what do they call themselves?'

'Farrant's group calls itself New Vision apparently.'

'Sounds like an optician's. And how do they differ from Martyn Shaw's lot?'

Ray shrugged. 'Apart from the fact that they still see Morgan as the true Prophet, I've no idea. No one at Sommers was very forthcoming.'

'And your little chat with Katie, what did you glean from that?'

'That she remembers a hell of a lot more than she thinks she does. I want to talk to Beckett, and her parents, get them to agree to me taking her out to the site of the original chapterhouse. See if anything else springs to her mind once she's there.'

He pushed his plate aside. The food was very good but he found it hard to take any pleasure in it without feeling guilt. Two families had lost children and, if Ray's calculations were right, then a third would be taken tonight. He found it hard to think of anything else.

'We know the third location,' George said thoughtfully. 'Have there been similar links with the abductions?'

Ray shook his head. 'So far, no.' He got up and pulled an A–Z map of Mallingham from the bookshelves. They cleared the table and he laid it out, then fetched coloured marker pens from the office. 'Here, here and here,' he said. 'Warwick Street, Roger Joyce lived at 53. Barratt Road. That's over here, right across town. Phillip Abrahams was just eleven and he lived above the corner shop with his mum and brother. And Nathan Brown, the last of the three. St Augustine Road, which back then was a main road between rows of terraced streets with a church on one corner and a pub on the other.'

He took a different pen and marked the locations of the new abductions. 'And these' – he took a third marker – 'are where the bodies were found. St Leonard's Vicarage, the Fosse Cinema and here, the third one was found in a pub yard, laid out on one of the tables. Sarah and I drove by where it used to be the other night. More bloody redevelopment. Why the hell they never finish one lot before they pull something else down beats me.'

George gave him a shrewd look. 'Why is this last place so important?' he asked.

Ray laughed harshly. 'I grew up close to there. One

of the little back streets off the King Richard's Road. Ryman Street. There was a shop on the corner, Mrs Snow's. She was ancient even when I was a little kid, one of those old women who are born that way and go on for ever. My dad used to drink at the pub, Robin on the Green it was called, though the only green round there was the colour of the curtains. I suppose I felt like anyone else who has a violent act take place on their doorstep. I felt possessive about the place I grew up in and to have something like that happen, to have to go and interview my old neighbours, my dad's old friends. It was a strange thing and yes, I guess it made Nathan's death more personal even than the other two.'

They gazed at the map, trying to discern a pattern, something that the killer saw but they did not. George even tried measuring distance, both actual and by road – examined the geometry of it all – but there was nothing discernible.

When will it happen? Ray asked himself, aware of the knot of dread that tightened his stomach and turned his insides to water. He thought of Beckett. He'd be asking the self-same thing, trying to position his officers to cover the most ground. Knowing that even the best cover would be too thin and imprecise.

He knew he had to do something. To join Beckett's force, even though one more pair of eyes would make little difference in a town the size of Mallingham.

As though he read Ray's thoughts, George went and fetched their coats. 'Keep your mobile on,' he said, 'and call in at least once an hour.'

Ray nodded.

'We'll meet back here at six tomorrow morning.'

Mallingham at night was like any town, a place of shadows and yellow lights. Darkness smoothed the torn edges of a community that was having the heart ripped out of it, physically and now emotionally. Mallingham had come late to the redevelopment by destruction approach adopted by the town planners. Leicester had endured this in the 1970s. Row upon row of Victorian terraces ripped apart, giving way to concrete and high-rise, despite the lessons of the previous decade that communities originally established at ground level could not survive being turned on end and thrust into the sky. The planners in the nearby city had learned their lessons and by the 1990s had begun to make the most of what they had instead of giving way to the wholesale destruction of the past. The tendency to pull down real eighteenth century in order to rebuild the mock type had been abandoned and now Victorian factories and ancient churches were seen as something to be treasured and reused rather than knocked down in the name of progress.

Mallingham had yet to learn that lesson and corporate vandalism was still the order of the day. At the turn of every road a new pile of rubble had appeared. The planners had preserved the odd building, like St Leonard's Church, and here and there enterprising souls had even tried planting gardens on long-abandoned plots. Trees sprang up in the midst of brick-strewn lots and a children's playground stood alone, complete with new slides and climbing frames, although the children it was meant to entertain had now been moved to new estates on the edge of town.

Ray drove to the police station to talk to Beckett. Outside, the media had gathered in force and television cameras all but blocked the street.

Ray did a U-turn, mounting the pavement at the end of the road and attracting unwanted attention from the crowd. He drove off at speed, far more speed than was wise in narrow streets where cars were parked on either side and speed bumps, new and red-brick-edged, seemed to have been breeding. He called Beckett on his mobile from two streets away.

'Where are you?' Beckett wanted to know.

Ray told him.

'Stay put, I'll get someone to bring me over.' He was with Ray fifteen minutes later. 'They're picking me up again on their next sweep,' he said as the patrol car drove slowly away. 'What happened down among the crackpots?'

'At Sommers House? Very little of any use, I suspect. Did you get my message about Farrant and his splinter group?'

'The New Vision lot? As it happened, they contacted us. By fax if you please, from their solicitor.'

'And what did it say, this brief from their brief?'

It was a poor attempt at humour, but Beckett understood. He smiled slightly. 'That they deny any association with these deaths and emphasize the law-abiding nature of their membership. Nothing you wouldn't expect.'

Ray nodded. 'I told Bryn Jones to make a similar statement,' he said. 'Other than that, I advised them to sit tight and do nothing.'

'Hope they take the advice. Something tells me Farrant's lot won't.'

Beckett sighed, and slumped down in the seat of Ray's car, his unbelted raincoat pulled around him. Ray could see in the half-light that he had not shaved.

'You had any sleep lately?'

'Not much. The PM reports have come in. They've rushed them through, the preliminary findings at least, we're still waiting on toxicology.'

'Asphyxia following sedation,' Ray guessed. 'The kids don't struggle. He puts them to sleep, takes samples of their blood, cuts off a few strands of hair and then smothers them with whatever's handy. Last time it was a cushion. Blue, if I remember correctly.'

Beckett nodded. Ray wasn't looking at him and he felt the movement rather than saw. He was staring out of the windscreen towards the end of the road. A warehouse had been demolished and the road end, which had once been blocked by a wall of red brick, now gave an unexpected view over the north of Mallingham.

'How many streets?' Ray said softly. 'How many houses and families and kids?'

Beckett said nothing. 'If you're cruising round tonight, expect to be stopped,' he said. 'I've got road-blocks on all the main drags and police check-points everywhere I can spare the manpower. Extra men stationed around what was the Robin on the Green pub. You'd better warn your partner. I suppose he's out here too?'

Ray nodded.

The patrol car prowled back along the deserted street and Beckett opened the door, ready to go. He seemed to be about to speak, but changed his mind. Ray watched as he got into the other car and it moved slowly away. What more was there to say? he thought.

As Ray left Mallingham he realized that he was not alone. At first he thought the bike following him must simply be someone setting off for the early shift at work, but something about the way the rider kept a fixed distance between them and resisted all opportunity to overtake once they'd reached the dual carriageway made him think again.

The bike was old. Not one of the plastic-coated superbikes that all looked the same to Ray. He lowered the window, listening closely to the roar of the engine as it cut through the damp air. He thought at first that the bike was a big single, the slow lazy thump of the engine totally unlike the screaming revvy engines of its modern cousins, but no, he decided, it was an old twin, even strokes and a low, grating roar to the exhaust note. Ray had owned several bikes in his youth, been really keen until his wife's nagging forced him to turn in his bike keys for a nice respectable car.

He slowed down deliberately and watched in his rear-view as the rider did the same, the engine note changing as he dropped the gear down a notch, then matching his speed again as Ray accelerated away.

They reached the outskirts of town. There were two

major roundabouts where the A46 met the narrower A roads off to Thurmaston and Syston and Ray deliberately hesitated before moving onto the first of them. The bike had anticipated his move. He held back, advancing slowly, waiting for Ray to pull off. This early in the morning there was little traffic and Ray decided to wait him out.

The biker drew level in the other lane and for a moment Ray was able to see more clearly the young man in dark leathers, his helmet visor pulled right down, before he accelerated away, leaving Ray with an impression of red and chrome and a roar of sound.

Since that night he had avoided the sun and kept himself in the darkened places where his soul could breathe. He had been the special one, the chosen, the cherished, protected by the faithful, and now his time had come and the journey could begin.

The night that his mentor had died he had known it even as it happened, felt the strength of another soul flow into his own and another heart beating. And he had known that it was time to complete the circle and to make things whole. He had tried to show them, to call the faithful to abandon their false prophets and come back to the truth, but the response had been small. Other powers kept his words from being understood.

So now he painted it large upon the walls of the room, taking time to do it well. The Prophet's words. Pigment and blood to give them power and worth.

'Man is like an angel falling.'

Chapter Seventeen

By seven-fifteen there were two possibles. One was a fifteen-year-old girl whose mother had reported her missing having found her bed empty. Beckett felt that this could probably be discounted and waited confidently for the news that she had been found safe and well after sneaking out to see a boyfriend or sleeping over at a friend's. None the less, he dispatched Emma Thorn to deal with the distraught parent.

A few minutes later a call came in which Beckett knew must be the one. There was an eleven-year-old boy by the name of Simon Ellis whose mother started work at eight and to get there on time left home at half-past six. A neighbour went in daily, just before seven, to make sure that he was awake and getting ready for school, and Simon then walked to school later with the neighbour's own son. The last few days she had been driving them there and picking them up again in the afternoon.

This morning the neighbour had knocked on the door at ten to seven and been appalled to find it unlocked. She had gone inside. And what she found left her in no doubt that Simon had gone.

'Someone followed me,' Ray told George as they made tea. 'Someone on a motorbike.'

'You're sure?'

'Oh yes. They made no attempt to hide it. They kept tight behind me from Mallingham to the outskirts of town. Then I pulled over and they sped past.'

'Then it might have been coincidence.'

'It might. I wrote the reg number down anyway. And the bike was unusual. Vintage-looking, not one of these plastic things you see now. I think it was red, though it was hard to tell in the dark.'

George frowned thoughtfully. 'Nothing else?' he asked.

Ray shook his head.

'I spoke to Dignan on the way in.'

'Who?' Ray asked. 'Oh, your old boss. I'd forgotten I was now a trainee spook. What did he want?'

'To know what progress we'd made.'

'Funny time to call you.'

'He knows I don't sleep well. Neither does he. I told him I'd be sending a report, which I'll prepare this morning. He's arranged a courier.' He paused to pour the tea and sat down with a tired sigh. 'I must be getting old. I'll be here to set Miss Leavers on the right track anyway.'

'Who? Oh, Rowena. Yes, that would be helpful.'

'Tell me about her. What she's like. What do I expect?'

Ray frowned. 'Five eight, five ten. Sarah's height. Dark hair, she wears it long, and green eyes. Nice shape and she wears an ankle bracelet, or at least she did last time I saw her. She seems pleasant, and if she's been working with Martha I'd guess she's efficient. Martha expects no less.'

Jane Adams

He closed his eyes and leaned back in his chair, wishing he could go to bed for even a short while, though he knew that if he once gave in to sleep then he'd not wake again for a long time. And Beckett would call. He knew Beckett would call.

Chapter Eighteen

Beckett's call came at nine o'clock, a brief conversation giving Ray the address and the name of the boy, Simon Ellis. That was all. Ray arrived at the crime scene at nine forty, having negotiated the aftermath of the rush hour – reps and lorries headed out on the A46.

The flats in Repton Street, Mallingham, had barely changed since Ray had lived not more than half a dozen streets away. They were built over shops, a supermarket, a launderette and a greengrocer, concrete stairs leading from the back of the shops to a balcony shared by all four of them.

Beckett had left word and Ray was guided through the cordon and taken to the flat. A crowd had gathered, inevitably. It was unnaturally silent, watching, as Ray crossed the line, and the press had already arrived, alerted by Beckett's departure from the police station. They called for statements. Shouted questions that Ray chose to ignore. He could feel the speculation in their collective gaze. It prickled between his shoulder blades and lifted the hairs on the back of his neck. With his scars and the publicity of the Pierce affair, with its high-profile drugs seizure and accusations of police corruption, Ray's was not an unknown face. His hopes of a quiet retirement away from the public eye seemed to have been dashed already.

The officer on duty outside the front door directed Ray into the child's bedroom, where Beckett was waiting for him. He said nothing as Ray stepped over the threshold and stood still, taking in the blue walls and football posters now defaced with a madman's graffiti. The Eye of God gazed down upon them from a circle six feet across and beneath it, written in strong, flowing script, the words, 'Man is like an angel falling.'

'Someone wants to be sure we get the point,' Ray commented softly.

'There was nothing like this the last time?'

'No. Nothing at all. Harrison Lee kept a low profile. He didn't need to shout about what he was doing, it wasn't necessary.'

'Not necessary?'

Ray shook his head. 'Lee was a man on a mission. Oh, we never figured out what it was and as far as Lee was concerned it was none of our business. He certainly did not go in for this kind of . . . exhibitionism. How was the boy taken?'

'Out of the front door, we think. No forced entry and nothing to indicate a struggle.'

'Lee drugged his victims. This one probably does the same.'

'The mother goes to work at six thirty. The next-door neighbour comes in about fifteen minutes later to make sure he's up. He's not there. Normally, she'd let herself in, she had a key. A few days ago her bag was stolen and she lost her keys. They hadn't had another cut yet.'

'Convenient for someone,' Ray commented harshly. 'Any description of the thief?'

'Male, white, early twenties and with dark hair. It was snatched on the street.'

'And you can't afford to rule out a connection. That this whole thing was pre-planned.'

'No, of course not. Someone knew the boy's routine. Each of their routines. They knew that Ian was allowed to run home alone. That Tim would worry about his lost dog. That the neighbour had a key.' He shook his head. 'The question is, how long ago was it planned?'

'How long ago did Lee know that he was dying? What visitors did he have in the last weeks?'

'There were none. Not in the entire time he was in prison. No visitors, no letters. He made no calls. The prison visitors found him unwelcoming and seemingly unconcerned. He was moved about a great deal in the early days, transferred from one prison to the next. No one wanted him for long. He caused trouble, not because he was violent or disruptive in the normal way. But I've talked to several prison officers now and three of the governors. They say that he had a way of setting people against each other. Unnerving the inmates and the officers. They were all glad to see the back of him.'

'But he was longer at Ashenfield?'

Beckett nodded. 'It's as if that's where he wanted to be. When he was transferred there he settled down. There were no more complaints and no more disruptions. Of course, the governor puts that down to their regime, reckons it had a good influence, but it makes you wonder.'

'He wanted to be close to Mallingham.' Ray frowned. 'What's in Mallingham that's so precious? There are

111

children everywhere and nothing at all to single these three out from a million others. Katie wasn't here. The chapter had destroyed itself. I don't get it.'

'The killer,' Beckett said quietly. 'He was here. Lee passed on the torch.'

'Or sent his soul,' Ray said drily.

'Is that what *they* believe?'

'Truthfully,' Ray said, 'I don't know. They say that's what Lee believed and maybe that's the important thing. Especially if the killer believed it too. That was his cue to begin.'

Beckett shook his head. 'I still don't get it. If whatever Lee set out to do was incomplete, then why didn't this other bastard carry on? Let the heat die down and then finish.'

'Because Lee *wasn't* dead. If Bryn and Irene and their friends are right and Lee planned to ... possess ... someone, for want of a better expression, then it had to be after Lee had died. Alive, he was just another man. Dead and resurrected as someone else ...' He shrugged helplessly, turning to gaze once more at the eye within the circle and the finely traced script. 'Then I lose it,' he said. 'We should talk to Martyn Shaw.'

'Difficult, seeing as he's in Chicago.'

'There are planes.'

'And I can just see the department funding that.'

'And we should see this Farrant and his group. If they're followers of Morgan, then they must have been around when Lee killed those children. Someone must have known what the hell he was up to.'

As they turned to leave the room, Beckett said, 'Not

everyone's keen for me to have you on board, not even informally. They reckon you make waves.'

'I can guess what's being said. There's only one thing worse than a bent pig and that's one who gets caught. Only one thing worse than a corrupt pig and that's one who blows whistles. Like I give a damn any more. Is it causing you problems?'

Beckett looked around him, gestured angrily back at Simon's room. 'You mean compared to this?' he said. 'The Pierce case is up in court next month?'

Ray nodded. 'And is *that* a problem?'

'Not for me.'

'Good, then you can tell your superiors that their objections are duly noted. Now can we get on with the job in hand?'

Beckett smiled grimly. 'I'd as soon,' he said. 'Oh, Katie wants to see you. She's been pestering her parents to take her to see what's left of the house and they've agreed as they're here. They go home tonight, so . . .'

'Great minds,' Ray commented.

'Pardon?'

'I'd been wondering how to convince them to go out there with me. Thought if anything could awaken memories it would be that place. You say they're leaving tonight?'

'No reason for them to stay. We know where they are if we need to talk to her again, but frankly I think it's a dead end.'

'What do you think made her come all the way here? Now, I mean?'

'I don't know. Don't have kids myself and can't

113

pretend I understand them. Something she saw or heard or read in the media triggered buried memories and caused her to dream. I don't know. Fortunately, I'm not paid to know, I leave that to the shrinks. Do you have kids?'

Ray shook his head. 'No. But I don't think you should dismiss Katie.'

'You believe in this dream thing?' Beckett sounded disapproving. 'You think Lee called her from his death-bed? I thought you were more down-to-earth than that.' He sounded angry, unreasonably so, and must have realized this, because he apologized at once. 'No offence. I'm sorry.'

'None taken, and, on the belief score, I guess I'll keep an open mind. There are things I've seen and felt that, well, that have left me a bit doubtful about what is and isn't possible. One thing I've learned, it often doesn't matter what I believe half as much as what other people do. People act on their beliefs.'

Beckett nodded. 'I take your point,' he said. He glanced at his watch and sighed. 'Press call in an hour.'

'Oh, joy! Before you go, I was followed home last night. It might be nothing but I'm pretty sure I saw the same bike this morning on my way here.'

'Bike?'

'Motorbike. Bright red and from what I saw this morning a lot of chrome. The rider was dressed in leathers and a black helmet, pretty standard, but the machine was something else. Looked like a vintage Brit.'

'You get the number?'

Ray reached into his pocket and gave Beckett the slip

of paper on which he'd scribbled the registration. Beckett was frowning as though something had come to mind.

'What?' Ray demanded.

'At Lee's funeral. Or rather, just after it. There were complaints about a bike, a red and chrome vintage machine with straight-through pipes riding through the cemetery. Might be coincidence, but . . .' He tapped the piece of paper. 'I'll have it run through PNC. Give Katie a call, won't you?'

Ray promised that he would and together they returned through the cordon, the moment captured on film by at least a dozen photographers. Once more, Ray ignored the shouted questions, while Beckett paused to remind them of the press call and that there would be a statement then.

Ray drove away, putting several streets between himself and the crime scene before pausing to use the phone. He called Katie's hotel and arranged to pick the family up in half an hour, wondering what the visit to the site of the old chapterhouse would produce.

Chapter Nineteen

Mitch had phoned George. The media machine had reached Sommers House big-time. They were camped out at the gate and although they had not tried to come onto Sommers land no one could leave the house without being filmed or photographed.

'It's unnerving to switch on the television and see yourself,' she told George. 'Is there anything we can do?'

'Nothing, I'm afraid, and any attempt to force them to leave is more likely to make things worse. Do you have food? Supplies? Do any of you need to try and get out?'

Mitch laughed, though she sounded strained. 'We've got enough to withstand a siege,' she said. 'Irene's been stocking up ready for the conference season to start. You should see our freezers.'

'Then sit tight until it's all over. Try to ignore them. At least they're not actually on your doorstep.'

'No,' Mitch agreed. 'I suppose it could be worse. Dad phoned. He wants me to go home.'

'Do you want to?'

'No. But I don't want them to worry either.'

'There's no way to avoid that, Mitch. I'm sorry. You have a choice to make here.'

'I know. I've made it. I have to stay, but I'm scared, George. The older members have told me what it was like the last time. How long do you think this will go on for?'

'No way of knowing, I'm afraid. Just sit tight and say nothing, and try not to worry too much. I'll give your father a call and tell him it's better if you stay. If you leave, the media will follow you too and I can't see Patrick wanting them hanging round the Grange.'

The thought of her father dealing with the press made Mitch laugh. 'He'd threaten to set the dogs on them.'

'That I'd like to see. Beck can't make it down the drive without help these days and Riker would just lick them into submission. Look, I'll give you a call later, OK?'

As he put the phone down he wondered if Dignan had had it tapped. He assumed so. Rowena was regarding him with interest.

'Martha told me all about those people.'

'Martha may be a little biased.'

'Can you blame her?'

'No. No, I can't blame her, but from what I've seen of Sommers House, they're about as threatening as you are.'

'Is it true they have kids out there?'

'Yes, there are several children, and they are loved and cherished from what I could see.'

The look Rowena gave him was more expressive than words. George sighed. The welfare of the children was something the media would be sure to focus on and public opinion would be behind them if Rowena was anything to go by. He thought grimly of the scandals at Cleveland and Orkney, of the Satanic abuse cases that had swept the United States and the mishandling of the children who'd survived Waco, and he felt a moment of real dread. The children at Sommers House had seemed happy. There were enough victims in this business already without adding to the list.

At Sommers House the adults had gathered to discuss what could be done.

'If George thought we could do any more to help ourselves, he would have said,' Mitch told them. 'I think he's right and we've just got to hope they catch this man soon.'

Bryn nodded. 'I wish that Martyn would contact us,' he said.

They had sent messages to the Prophet via his second-in-command, Charles Marriott, but so far there had been no word from the Prophet. Mitch could see that Bryn was feeling this absence painfully.

'And what could the Prophet tell us that's so different?' she asked him gently. 'We all know that this has nothing to do with us and in time everyone else will know that too.'

No one said anything. The depression in the room was palpable.

'Look,' Mitch went on. 'Contact the Prophet again. Maybe Charles Marriott didn't tell him how bad it really was.'

'Mitch is right,' Amy said. 'Bryn, call Martyn again instead of sitting here wondering why he hasn't contacted us. Do it now.'

Bryn nodded slowly. 'Of course,' he said. 'You're

quite right, and the important thing is to keep our spirits up. We know this has nothing to do with any of us. It's only a matter of time before everything is back to normal again.'

'This other group,' Mitch asked, 'the one led by Farrant. Do you think that they might be involved?'

Bryn looked at her as though she had said something absurd. 'In what way? You think one of them could be the murderer?'

'It's possible.' Mitch shrugged. 'They were around when Lee and Morgan were in charge. They don't accept Martyn's right to be the Prophet.'

'That doesn't make them killers,' Irene said gently.

'What was Lee trying to do?' Mitch asked. 'Surely you must have some idea.'

'Why should we know?' Bryn asked her quietly. 'Mitch, the man was insane. It's sad but it's true, and unfortunately sometimes people with the sorts of personality problems Lee had become attracted to groups like ours. All religions have had their fanatics. Their madmen. That's why our screening process is so careful these days. No one wants another Lee.'

'And Morgan?' Mitch asked. 'He killed himself and so did ten other people. That's not exactly a sane act either, is it?'

'Morgan wasn't mad,' Irene said – a little angrily, Mitch thought. 'Morgan was our First Prophet. A great man. He chose to die because he felt himself shamed by Lee's actions.'

'And those with him?' Mitch pushed on. 'There were two dead children that night and one who only just survived. Irene, I'm committed to this community, to what it's doing here and now, but there are things I've never understood. I'm having an even harder time with them now and one of my main problems is Morgan.'

'Daniel Morgan was a great and spiritual man,' Irene retorted angrily. Then she calmed. 'Doubts are natural, Mitch, especially at times of crisis. You should meditate on your doubts and, when the Prophet calls, talk to him.'

Mitch nodded. This was not the first time she had questioned the group about Morgan and expressed her feelings about him. For Mitch, the Eyes of God was the organization as it was now. Led by Martyn Shaw. A religion that sought to integrate science and spirituality but without the submersion of the individual. For the first time since joining the chapter at Sommers House, Mitch felt uncertain. Felt that they were not being wholly truthful with her.

She looked back at Irene, then turned her gaze to the altarpiece painted on the north wall of the room. A triptych, beautiful and detailed, depicting man and angels, the arts, science and religion, and the Prophet Martyn Shaw.

Beneath it, the words 'Man is like an angel falling.'

Chapter Twenty

The old chapterhouse was set in about an acre of land. It had been abandoned since the explosion, though apparently the Eyes of God still held the deeds. Pulling up on the grass verge at the side of the road, Ray wondered just how much an acre of building land this close to Charnwood Forest would be worth these days.

The road was narrow, a B road running through woodland and close to a golf course, membership of which still had all the exclusivity of a gentleman's club. Ray recalled interviewing the neighbours at the time. The closest house was fifty yards down the road, but it had been occupied by a pair of widowed sisters with little better to do all day than watch the comings and goings at what was then called the Markham house.

The sisters had liked the inhabitants of the Markham house. In fact they had been frequent visitors, calling in for tea at least once in the week, and they reported that they had always been made welcome, even when their visits had been unexpected. A dozen people had lived there, but there had been no children resident. Those who had died must have arrived the day of the explosion and Ray knew that at least two of the regular inhabitants had been away at the time, even though their names had initially been released by the cult as being among the dead.

The gate was rusted but still solid, though what looked to be the growth of eleven years had all but covered the fence and threatened to jam the hinges closed. It was just as well, he thought, that they had arrived in February, when only the hardiest of evergreens and the odd snowdrop were making their presence felt. In the height of summer the land would be like a jungle as nature reclaimed its own.

It was the first time that Katie's parents had seen the place. They watched as Katie poked around in the undergrowth, trying to make out the ground plan. She had found a long stick in the hedge and prodded along what was left of the walls.

'This place must have been enormous,' Lisa Fellows commented.

'It was,' Ray confirmed. 'Though I never saw it in the flesh as it were. Only photographs of it after it had gone. The old ladies who used to live over there' – he pointed to the house down the lane – 'they'd been here all their lives and knew the original owners, the Markhams. They had photographs of the place from the time it was built right up to the time it was blown to kingdom come. I heard they both died a year or two afterwards. The shock couldn't have done them much good. They were both as old as Methuselah.'

'What happened to the photographs?' Guy Fellows asked.

'I don't know. We had some copied for the official report, but I expect the rest went to the sisters' next of kin.' He frowned trying to recall their names. 'Albert,' he said. 'The Albert sisters.'

Katie was calling to them and they went over to where she was standing, at the rear of where the house had been.

'Was the kitchen here?'

Ray thought about it. 'I'd guess it must have been. There was a basement, wine cellar or something. I remember the steps down to it were still intact. Steps and a bit of wall.' He borrowed Katie's stick and poked around beneath elder bushes which had invaded what had once been a scullery. The Belfast sink lay half embedded in the floor. 'Somewhere about here,' he said. 'Though it's difficult to picture it after all this time. Pity we couldn't have dug up a ground plan from somewhere.'

'Where was Katie found?' Guy Fellows asked.

Ray frowned. 'If the back scullery was here and the kitchen through there . . . Look, there's the odd quarry tile sticking out of the ground.' He shook his head. 'Somewhere over there.'

'Over here?' Lisa crossed to where he was pointing.

'I'm not sure. A little to your left . . .'

Katie rolled her eyes at them, wandering back towards the front of the house and leaving them to their reconstruction. Her father had joined in by now, pacing the area with a professional air, trying to estimate the size of the kitchen and the scullery beyond. She wandered back through ghostly living rooms, finding the tiles from what had been the hall. Fragments of stained glass from the blue and yellow window that had decorated the front door.

And then the sound that came out of nowhere, shattering the peace, and Katie began to run, not away from the angry cracking roar but towards it.

Jane Adams

Ray and Katie's parents watched in horror as the red and chrome machine pulled up beside the gate and she climbed on board. The rider handed her an open-faced helmet and she pulled it on. With that the bike took off, carried on a wave of sound.

Chapter Twenty-One

Ray and the Fellowses ran to the gate, but the bike had already vanished around the bend in the road. The car was parked fifty yards away, at the only place where the grassy verge was wide enough to keep it off the narrow road. They headed for it at once.

Once in the car Ray handed the mobile phone to Guy and told him to call Beckett. He drove as fast as he dared down the lane, and bends that should have been treated with respect he took at sixty, feeling the wheels slip on the muddy road. He couldn't believe that he had been so stupid – an illogical thought, since he could not have known that this would happen. Had the biker followed them here? He was sure he would have seen him or, in the quiet of the countryside, at least have heard him way off in the distance. And yet the sheltered garden with its tall trees and muffling undergrowth had probably blocked far more sound than he had realized and the bike had approached fast, skidding to a halt at the gate. Even when they had heard the sound of its clipped pipes it had given them little warning.

There was no sign of it now.

Guy was shouting into the phone's mouthpiece at Beckett. In the back, Lisa was crying softly. When they reached the crossroads two miles from the house, Ray stopped the car and got out, taking the phone with him.

He stood in the centre of the crossroads, turning slowly, seeing nothing in any direction.

'What the hell happened?' Beckett demanded.

'Guy's just told you. The bike pulled up, Katie got on and they rode away. It was the same bike that followed me.'

'You're certain?'

'Like I told you. It's unmistakable. Question is, who the fuck is he?'

'Get back to the hotel,' Beckett ordered. 'We've managed to keep the girl out of the media so far, I'd like to keep it that way.'

Ray agreed. 'The reg number I gave you. Any joy?'

'Phoney,' Beckett said. 'I'm sorry, Ray, we seem to have drawn another blank.'

At Sommers House they were talking to the Prophet. Most of the community had crowded into the media room, which housed their video-conferencing equipment. Martyn Shaw was horrified at what was happening.

'Marriott said that you had been concerned about the murder of a boy in Mallingham,' he said. 'He gave me no indication that there was a connection to Lee or the other murders.'

'We've been advised to keep inside and wait until it's over,' Bryn told him. 'It's good advice, but it's very hard. Every time we turn on the television there's something about us on the news. Pictures of the house, library footage of Harry Lee's trial. It isn't good for any of us and it's especially hard on the children.'

'It must be. Bryn, you said you spoke to one of the original investigators. Was he helpful?'

'He's trying to be. His name's Ray Flowers and he's now retired, but they've got him in as an adviser. He's done his best to be sympathetic, but there isn't much he can do. And look at it from his point of view – we could all be as guilty as Lee.'

'He wanted to talk to you,' Mitch put in hastily.

'The Prophet doesn't want to be bothered by him,' Bryn told her sharply. 'Martyn, we can handle it. We're just glad you're there and out of it all.'

'But I'm not, Bryn. You are all a part of my community. My congregation. What affects you affects me. Mitch, I'm quite willing to talk to the policeman if he thinks it would help. I've nothing to hide.'

Mitch nodded. 'Thank you,' she said. But beside her she was aware that Bryn's body was tense and she could feel his anger.

Martyn Shaw was speaking to them again. 'Could you come here, all of you, until it blows over? There's room at the guesthouse. It might be a bit cramped, but I'm sure we could manage. If you don't have funds we could arrange for them to be wired to your account. I don't like the thought of you facing this alone.'

Bryn shook his head. 'We've discussed this,' he said. 'If we can find a quiet way of getting the families with children away then we're going to do that. This is our home and the rest of us will stay. We won't be driven out.'

*

Beckett, Ray and Katie's parents had returned to the hotel. Guy Fellows was furious. With him mostly, Ray figured, seeing as he was closest to hand. Beckett was doing his best to calm the situation. Lisa Fellows was still crying, though her tears had slowed now and Ray could see that anger was about to take their place. She was a mother who had twice lost her child.

Guy Fellows wanted to go public, to launch an appeal on the next news bulletin. Go to the papers, the radio, anything that might help. Beckett was having none of it. He was of the opinion that Katie must have known the motorcyclist and tended to think that the whole thing had been set-up. The biker had known exactly where she was going to be.

'Did she make any calls from the hotel? Have any kind of contact? Did she have a boyfriend that you maybe didn't approve of?'

Lisa Fellows shook her head. 'Katie didn't make any calls. There was no boyfriend. There was nothing like that.'

'We'll have the hotel phone records checked just in case,' Beckett told them. 'It's possible that you didn't know. That she called from her own room or even from the lobby.'

'Are you calling my wife a liar?' Guy shouted.

'Not your wife. No.'

It took a moment for Guy to realize what Beckett had said. 'You think Katie . . .'

Beckett sighed. 'Look at it calmly for a moment, Mr Fellows. How many kidnappers use a motorbike, carry a spare helmet and just stop for their victim to get on?'

Guy was stunned into silence.

'She wouldn't do that to us,' Lisa said. 'Not knowing what we've just been through. There's more to it than that. I just know.'

Beckett got up, ready to leave, and Ray did the same. 'I'll be sending Emma Thorn to take your statements,' Beckett said, 'and she'll give you her contact number so you can reach her any time. Right now, I'm afraid that's the best I can do.'

They walked off together, leaving the Fellowses to comfort one another. Ray paused in the hotel lobby.

'I think it's the boy she talked about. The one who saved her life last time.'

'Proof or hunch?'

Ray shrugged. 'It just makes a kind of sense. I think you're right that she either knows or knew him. What I'm not so sure of is that she's safe.'

'He saved her life last time. Why should he hurt her now? That's assuming you're right.'

Ray shook his head. 'I don't know,' he said. 'I'm just wondering what he saved her for.'

Chapter Twenty-Two

'I've had our new secretary write herself a contract,' George told Ray when he returned to the office. 'I think she'll work out very well.'

Ray slumped down in one of the chairs and closed his eyes. 'Nice to know something is,' he said.

'Tell me.'

Ray filled George in on the events of his day and on Beckett's views of the situation. George in turn told him about Mitch.

Ray was profoundly depressed. The post-mortems on the first two victims suggested they had died within twelve to fifteen hours of their abduction. Time was almost up for the third boy, Simon Ellis.

'They never found where Lee took the boys, did they?'

Ray shook his head. 'And he never told. To be honest, George, it wasn't good policework that implicated Lee, it was an anonymous tip-off. It must have come from inside the organization, but no one ever confessed. Lee was brought in, his place was searched and some of the kids' clothes were found there. What clinched it was a blood stain about the size of a two-pence piece on one of his shirts. We questioned him and he confessed within hours. I remember, though, it was as if he always intended to confess, just wanted to get the timing right. He kept glancing at his watch, as if he had a nervous tic of some sort, and telling us "all in good time" in that prissy, cultured voice of his.

'Then he confessed. I wasn't there for that. It was about an hour and a half after the chapterhouse blew up and by that time I was on the scene.'

'Lee knew what they had planned then?'

'Either that or Lee planned it all along with Morgan. I never did buy the mass-suicide bit, though, and Katie's description of being given something to drink that made her sleepy makes me buy it even less.'

'They might still have been willing. Those in the Heaven's Gate cult took part in assisted suicides. They drugged themselves first and someone finished it by asphyxiating them. The drug might just have been to make it easier.'

Ray shook his head. 'I don't buy it,' he repeated. 'I talked to a lot of the surviving members afterwards and none of them could believe it either. Suicide just didn't seem their style. I even met Martyn Shaw.'

'I didn't know that.'

Ray nodded. 'It was before Morgan's papers were released and he was declared the new Prophet. I liked him. I liked all of them. They weren't obsessed and they weren't controlling, like Mitch's lot out at Sommers House . . . You know what I'm saying?'

George nodded. 'I've been trying to explain that to Patrick,' he said. 'But it isn't easy. Why would Morgan and Lee want to murder their own followers? You believe that Katie's right and Morgan didn't die?'

'Yes, I do. I also think that if we knew exactly who *did* die that night, we'd be a hell of a lot closer to under-

131

standing the rest, but there weren't ever accurate lists of membership back then. People would join and then drift off, and of course many of them neglected to come forward when we appealed. Embarrassed, I suppose. Martyn Shaw seems to have made the whole thing far more exclusive, but back then it was something of a spiritual free-for-all.'

'So,' George asked, 'what next?'

'We've got a business to run. I keep having to remind myself that Beckett's the investigating officer and I'm just a civilian.'

'I can hold the fort here and you *are* working. My dearly beloved ex-boss is following your every move, you can be sure of that, so keep a note of your expenses.'

'Oh, well, the retainer will be useful.'

'They pay well. That's one thing to be thankful for.'

'Your friend, Patrick, you still going to bill him?'

'Of course. He'd expect no less. Ray, if Morgan didn't die, do you think he's our murderer?'

Ray shrugged. 'It had crossed my mind,' he said.

Chapter Twenty-Three

Katie and the motorcyclist had hidden in the trees at the side of the road and watched Ray and her parents drive by in the car. They had seen Ray get out at the crossroads and look all about him, then talk into the mobile phone. Finally they had watched him as he drove away. Katie could see Lisa crying in the back seat.

She had wanted to run to her, to tell her that it was all OK and that she shouldn't worry, but she was torn between anxiety about her parents and the bond she felt for this familiar stranger. Although he was weird, Katie decided. Really weird. The most solid thing about him seemed to be his bike leathers and helmet. The creature inside seemed far more difficult to define.

They had stood there in the woods until the biker was certain that Ray had gone away and Katie had complained that she was cold. Then he had ridden off with her again, towards town and then through the back streets of Mallingham and into a run-down lock-up garage. Inside was a second set of doors, though you'd have to have been looking for them, concealed as they were beneath the filthy floor. He opened them and Katie saw a ramp leading down. Absurdly, she was reminded of the Bat Cave or something equally surreal.

The ramp led to a basement. When the biker flicked

on the light, what Katie saw put everything else out of her mind.

Ray was preoccupied all evening, despite Sarah's attempts to distract him. The weather had turned filthy again after what had been a bright and frosty day. Now the rain was falling as though it never wanted to stop.

'What's nagging at you?' Sarah wanted to know.

'You mean apart from three dead boys and a missing girl?'

'You don't know the third one's dead, Ray.'

The look he gave her was full of despair.

'Is it always like this?'

'What do you think?' He spoke more sharply than she deserved and he apologized.

'That's all right, I can take it, but I asked you a question. What's nagging at you?'

'I don't know. A feeling, maybe, like when you can't remember if you locked the doors or turned off the gas. I'll talk to Beckett tomorrow, ask if I can go through Lee's statements.'

'I'm sure they're already doing that.'

'Maybe, but I was there. I have memories that can be jogged. Beckett and his team don't.'

The walls of the basement were decorated like the original temple of the Eyes of God. He was explaining the symbols to her, the stories the pictures told. His voice was soft and far away, and Katie was finding it hard to focus. Once she fell asleep, but she woke to find the thread of his conversation unbroken, as though she had been listening all the time.

'Long ago,' he said, 'the angels came to Earth. They mated with the daughters of men and heroes were born onto the Earth. They lived for hundreds of years and kept their bodies healthy and strong. The golden age of the gods, before the second flood and the destruction of the world. They knew that it was coming and most left, taking their stories and their songs with them back beyond the sky. But some remained. They loved the Earth and did not want to see it die, so they made an ark. Not like the ark of Noah, more like the ark of Utnapishtim in Sumeria, and they collected the seed of all the plants that grew and all the creatures of the Earth that crawled and flew and filled the oceans and the rivers, and they kept the seed safe until the flood had gone and the Earth could be re-formed.

'It was a different world then. One with greatness in it. Gods and magic and things we now hear only in legends. They had seeded the Earth, Katie, so long ago, our scientists have trouble even counting it. They made life come into a barren world and none of them wanted to see it die, even though their elders said that this was often the way of things and that they should let things be.

'They taught us that mankind is like the angels falling. Some fall a long, long way.'

Katie watched him as he moved around the room. There was no natural light and the illumination was provided by small spots set into the vaulted ceiling like so many stars. There were no furnishings apart from large cushions piled up on the floor. Katie sat down on these, watching the dark-haired man.

At the back of the big room Katie could glimpse two doors. One, he said, led through to the kitchen. One to the bathroom. She had used the bathroom earlier, but there had been no window and no other doors. She was afraid now, though fascinated. Wishing herself elsewhere and regretting her impulse to go with him.

'Will you let me go?'

He shook his head.

'Not ever?'

'Not yet, later . . . I don't know.'

He went through to the bathroom, leaving the door ajar, and she could hear him urinating. She crept to the basement entrance and tried the door, even though she had seen him lock it. His bike was parked close by. The smell of hot exhaust and oil was sharp in her nose.

She heard the toilet flush and water run into the bowl as he turned on the tap, and she crept back to her place on the cushions. She heard the water splashing as though he was taking time to wash, not just rinse, his hands and she wondered if she might be able to lock him in, though she couldn't remember seeing a lock on the outside of the door. And it still wouldn't solve the problem of how to get out. It might give her some time to look around though. She decided to try.

As she reached the door he came out. He'd removed his shirt.

'I . . . er . . . needed the bathroom,' she said.

He stood aside and as she passed him she caught sight

of his back reflected in the bathroom mirror. Other eyes stared back at her. Four images tattooed there and a fifth loosely sketched in waiting to be finished. Katie recognized one face. Ian Thomason, she had seen his picture in the papers. The image was fresh and new, unlike the other three, which were obviously older. At the edge of the boy's hair the skin was reddened as though irritated and there were faint signs of scabbing as it began to heal.

'Did you kill them?' Katie whispered.

The young man regarded her thoughtfully for a moment.

'What do you think?' he said.

Part Two

Chapter Twenty-Four

It was twenty-four hours since Simon Ellis had been abducted and Dave Beckett was no further on. He stared out of his office window frustrated by the lack of progress. Where was he? Was he still alive?

Across town, Katie's parents lay in bed both pretending to be asleep, each determined to let the other rest, until they could stand the deception no longer. Guy got up and dressed silently.

'You're going out again?'

He nodded. 'It's better than doing nothing. Stay here in case she calls,' he added, not realizing the irony in what he'd said.

At the scene of Simon Ellis's abduction a few hardy journalists still kept vigil, along with a couple of officers standing on the balcony outside the flat. The heavy rain had emptied the streets.

Inside the flat, someone had turned on the lights. They shone yellow in the grey dawn, a soiled beacon to welcome no one home.

Ray forced himself to eat breakfast with Sarah and they watched the television news. Nothing had happened overnight and the report simply rehashed the incidents of the day before.

In the papers there were photographs of Sommers House and also of himself and Dave Beckett. He had expected this, but still was not happy about it. One of the national papers had used a photograph of Ray from eleven years before, when he had attended Roger Joyce's funeral on behalf of the force. It was presented alongside a new picture of himself and Beckett leaving the police HQ in Mallingham. There was a report, outlining his background and explaining how he came by his injuries. Ray found himself projected as an old-fashioned copper fighting police corruption and getting fried for his troubles. He groaned and Sarah took the paper off him.

'Expect anything less, did we? Always were bloody naïve.'

He rubbed at his scarred face. A reflex these days whenever he was stressed.

'Hope springs eternal, I suppose.'

Sarah snorted rudely. 'Well,' she said, 'get yourself off then. You know you're only being polite.' She smiled at him sympathetically. 'Or are you just avoiding the inevitable?'

He got up and fetched his coat. 'I'll see you tonight,' he said.

Katie was sitting on the giant cushions eating breakfast and reading the morning papers. She didn't know whether to be relieved or sorry that there was no mention of her. Dave Beckett must be trying to keep her out of it.

'They'll be looking for you,' Katie told the biker. 'Aren't you afraid of getting caught?'

'He protects me. I won't be seen unless I want to be.'

'Don't be daft,' Katie told him bluntly with more courage than she felt. 'You went into a shop. You ride the noisiest bike I've ever heard. You can't just hide yourself.'

He said nothing. In the kitchen the electric kettle switched off. He stood up and suddenly Katie saw him standing in the kitchen though she had no recollection of having seen him cross the room. She looked around uncomfortably and wasn't hungry any more.

'What are you?' Katie demanded when he came back into the room.

'What do you want me to be?'

'Don't play games with me. It's not clever.' She bit her lip. She sounded like a petulant child and sensed that this was not the way to handle him. 'I don't understand,' she said finally. 'Who looks after you?'

He smiled. 'Man is like an angel falling,' he recited in his faraway sing-song voice. 'Some fall further than others, Katie, and I guess Harry Lee fell about as far as Lucifer himself.'

'Harrison Lee? He killed those boys? I thought he was dead. He can't be who takes care of you.'

'What's dead, Katie? What's it mean? Have you ever asked yourself that? Harry Lee said that death was like alchemy. A transmutation of the soul from one state to the next. It happens to all of us, many, many times.'

'Did you kill them?' Katie asked again. 'Those kids tattooed on your back?'

He thought about it for what felt like a long time. 'Maybe I did,' he said finally. 'What's certain is they died because of me.'

Chapter Twenty-Five

It had been a quiet day. Beckett had been away for most of it, leaving Ray to go through the records of Lee's interviews alone. Reading through brought back even more clearly the changing mood of the first investigation. The initial shock of the first death, then bewilderment and outrage, ending in desperation as the third child died. The fear that there would be more and the anxiety caused by such seemingly motiveless and random acts. As a police officer, Ray had always been grateful for a clear motive. It often made the tracking of a suspect so much easier. Not understanding the reasons behind the deaths took away initial leads and their subsequent developments. It was like working in a vacuum, nothing to push against and no air to breathe.

Then, Lee's arrest, the discovery of objects in his house that made direct connections to the crimes. The feeling almost of exultation as the evidence grew and they knew that all they needed was the confession to make it complete. Reading Lee's statements, Ray was reminded just how much the man had played with them. His glee as he forced them to wait for the confession he had already decided he would make, but on his own terms and in his own good time.

*

Katie's fear had given way to boredom. He had gone out for a time during the day, come back and fallen asleep. Then he had woken suddenly and, without saying a word to her, gone through to the kitchen and prepared food. It seemed to Katie that he continued with his life pretty much as though she was not there. It was hard in a place with no natural light to judge the time. Her watch told her one thing but the constant light levels, neither daytime bright nor night dark, confused her body and made her feel like she existed in eternal dusk.

'What's your name?' she had asked him, and he had looked at her strangely as though the idea made no sense.

'Call me Nathan,' he had said at last. It was the name of Lee's third victim.

'Is that your name?'

'It's . . . *a* . . . name. Call me Nate.'

She discovered that he had painted all of the images on the walls himself, as closely as he could remember to the originals in the temple of the Eyes of God.

'Did I ever go there?'

'I don't know. I only saw you that one time.'

'You told me to hide.'

He nodded slowly but did not seem inclined to discuss it further. He would, Katie feared, drift off into another of his reveries. To distract him she asked him how long it had taken for him to paint the images on the walls.

'Time,' he said. 'I don't know, a lot of time. At first, I didn't know how and I had to do and then redo them to get it right.'

'Why?'

Nathan looked at her with eyes that were distant and beautiful. 'To remind me,' he said.

Martha had gone to church, or rather the church had come to her. The gathering at St Leonard's had been spontaneous, word spreading from one person to the next until what had been a half-expressed idea became a reality.

For the first time in five years candles were lit where the altar had once stood and prayers were said in what had now been designated deconsecrated ground. Martha was amazed at how many had come. Faces she knew from her work on the streets or the missing persons register. Others that she did not recognize. They had come to pray, even those who rarely resorted to prayer, as if that act of coming together and willing acts undone could make it so.

Martha wept openly, and so did many more. They held candles and they stood in silence. From time to time someone would move to the front of the church and speak, saying out loud what so many felt.

'O God, why did you let this happen to our children?'

'O Lord Jesus, please let the police catch this madman before he kills again.'

'God, if you've got any power left in this world, help them catch this bastard.'

Martha listened, whispering her own prayers, knowing they would not be answered this time any more than they had been the last.

The door opened again. The media had got wind of this and had come to see. Martha moved deeper into the crowd. It was unlikely that anyone would recognize her after all this time, but she had no wish to take a chance. Journalists and cameramen crowded just inside the door at the back, huddled close, like uninvited guests at a funeral, come to pay their respects but with no right to approach the coffin.

Martha felt she could no longer bear what was going on or cope with the emotions that filled the old church. Trying hard not to draw attention to herself, she began to look for an escape route. Rowena stood by the door to the vestry, beckoning her. Gratefully, Martha slipped through the curtain and into the robing room.

'I've undone the little door,' Rowena said. 'The one in the basement.'

Martha kissed her gratefully. She had forgotten the old door to the boiler house. There was a way through from the choir school.

Martha followed Rowena out into the cold damp night. She breathed deeply. The air was fresh and it restored her a little. She turned towards the road, trying not to look at the pile of rubble where the child's body had lain.

'How is the job?' she asked, desperate for distraction.

'It's going to be good, I think. I've not seen much of your friend, but his partner's nice. Old-fashioned, very British, if you know what I mean.'

Martha nodded. 'Have they learned anything yet?'

'I don't know, Martha. As I told you, Ray's out a lot. He's working with the officer in charge this time, a DI Beckett, and trying to get information out of George is like trying to prise open fresh clams.'

Martha nodded again. She had expected nothing less. Ray and his partner were far too professional to gossip with someone they hardly knew.

She glanced up sharply and Rowena followed the direction of her gaze. Some way off the roar of a motor-cycle shredded the evening silence.

Chapter Twenty-Six

Edwin Farrant, representing New Vision, appeared on breakfast television. He was an elderly man with a neat white beard and a shock of silver hair. His jacket of heather-coloured Harris Tweed and grey flannel trousers lent him an air of old-style respectability that went well with his soft, educated voice.

The presenter was obviously impressed, Ray thought, as he watched the performance on Sarah's television. He felt better this morning. Against the odds, he'd managed to get some sleep. He had a strong suspicion that one of the sleeping pills from Sarah's medicine cabinet had gone into his last cup of tea, but he wasn't about to probe too deeply. Though he did wonder how long she'd had them and if sleeping pills had a sell-by date. He'd certainly never known her take one in the six months that he'd been involved with her.

'Would you buy a used car from this man?' Sarah intoned solemnly.

Ray shook his head. 'Used cars aren't his style. Phoney diplomas maybe. The kind of degree you can get through the post for fifty quid.'

Sarah laughed. 'Even so, you have to admit he's impressive-looking.'

Ray shrugged and eyed her suspiciously. 'He's got con man written all over him.'

'And Martyn Shaw hasn't?'

'No, I don't believe he has.'

Sarah raised a sceptical eyebrow as though frankly amazed that Ray should have time for any of it. 'So, what makes this one different?'

'Listen to him.' Ray gestured at the television.

'My group only want to be left in peace to pursue our own beliefs,' Farrant was saying. 'We've worked hard for acceptance, kept ourselves right out of the media gaze, and we were beginning to regain our respectability. To see all of that good work destroyed is unbearable.'

'Doesn't matter that three kids are dead as long as they're left alone,' Ray commented harshly.

'And yet,' the interviewer said, 'you've come on national television this morning, right into the public eye. That's hardly in keeping with your low profile, Mr Farrant.'

Farrant shifted in his seat so that he could look her straight in the eye. 'I have come here to show the public just how ordinary and how unashamed we are. We have done nothing. We are normal, law-abiding citizens who are proud to face the world because we know that we will be adjudged open and innocent.'

'From which you infer that the Eyes of God do have something to hide?'

'I have never said that. I would just point out that they have chosen to cut themselves off. Close their doors without statement or interview. You need only to look at the film of Sommers House to see what a climate of fear exists there. They will not even show their faces.' He paused dramatically and Ray's stomach tightened. He could guess what was coming next.

It came. With an expression full of concern and an eye to the camera, Farrant said quietly, 'And I need remind no one, I'm sure, that there are still children there, at Sommers House.'

Ray realized that he'd been holding his breath. He exhaled sharply. Farrant was no longer an object of the slightest humour. In that one statement he had upped the stakes for everyone concerned. 'Bastard!' he said.

Irene Jones had been troubled by dreams. In her dream she had walked with the Prophet beside the lake close to where he now had his headquarters. The sky was slate-grey with a weak sun trying to push through and the water reflected the deepest inky blue. Sunlight caught the waves as the wind whipped them into being, the silvered spray falling coldly on her skin.

It should have been a peaceful scene, but Irene was afraid. The lowering sky preyed upon her senses, depressing her mood despite its innate drama. She had the feeling that they were being watched and kept trying to glance back over her shoulder to see who was there, but each time she turned it was as though she whipped around full circle and found herself once more gazing out over the open water. Facing the darkening sky.

And then she saw him. A slight figure walking along the beach towards them. Dark hair and slight build, stripped to the waist despite the cold and barefoot, though he left no footsteps on the sand and shingle beach.

The Prophet was talking to her, though Irene could

not work out what he said. His voice, as so often in dreams, seemed to come from very far away. He did not seem to see the young man, though he was looking straight towards him. He seemed completely ignorant of his presence there on the beach. And all the time Irene could feel the pressure of invisible eyes upon her back. Piercing the skin with the strength of their focus and concentration.

She tried hard to tell the Prophet this. To point out the young man and warn him about the one who watched them. But her voice had gone, disappeared, and she no longer remembered how to speak. The young man had paused and turned to face the water. He did nothing to acknowledge them but simply waited until their path led them past him before turning again and walking back the way that they had come.

But it was the moment of transition that choked the breath from her. As she walked by and as he turned, she caught a glimpse of his narrow, pale-skinned back. The skin was red with blood oozing from it as though someone had carved it into a half-dozen or so complex designs. And as Irene tried to look closer, the bloody wounds began to coalesce to form the faces of children cut deep into the young man's back.

Tina finished the design and placed him between the mirrors so that he could judge the effectiveness of the results. Needle art worked in a delicate technique called water shading, which allowed a subtlety of tone and a silvery gradation through the greys that gave the young faces the life and expression that had now been denied them.

He nodded, satisfied. He rarely said much to her, it wasn't his way. He would bring the picture she was to use, explain how he wanted the work carried out and leave the rest to her. He never flinched, even when she worked close to the bone, and he never commended her on her work, though she knew that he was satisfied. That he returned time and time again told her that. But this was to be the last time.

'I can't do any more for you,' she said. 'I'm sorry, but I just can't.'

He had expected something like this. He said nothing, his back to her so that she could cover the new face with cling film held in place with masking tape.

He pulled on his shirt and turned to face her as he fastened it.

'You think that I'm the murderer.'

She laughed nervously. 'I don't know.'

'But you're afraid that I might be.'

She said nothing but she was clearly willing him to leave and wishing they were not alone.

'Why this? you're thinking, if I didn't kill them. Psychopaths collect trophies. This is my trophy. Is that what you're thinking?'

She shifted uncomfortably. He was between her and the door. Her gaze fell on the telephone sitting on the desk. He picked it up and handed it to her.

'Phone the police,' he said. 'Tell them about me. It doesn't matter.'

'They'll want to know why I didn't tell them before.'

'Why didn't you?'

She bit her lip and turned away without answering.

He left so quietly that it was several moments before she realized he'd gone.

Ray and Beckett stood in the incident room with a large-scale map spread on the table in front of them. Its twin hung on the wall, bright pins marking the sites of abductions and recoveries, past and present. They had laid this map out flat, trying to visualize the streets and the derelict lots as the killer might be seeing them. With Ray's help and a second, older map, Beckett attempted to superimpose the Mallingham of eleven years before onto this new one. So far it had given them no clue.

Outside the crowd had increased, the ranks of journalists swelled now by ordinary people. Families mostly. They had stood in silent vigil overnight but the morning had seen a change in mood. The chanting had begun about an hour before and could be heard even through closed windows: 'Find him, find him.' Ray was unsure whether they meant the killer or the missing child. The words growing louder then drifting back almost to a whisper, an ebb and flow of sound, sometimes falling silent for a moment before someone took it up again.

Inside the room Beckett and his assembled team did their best to ignore it, but it was the kind of input that the mind found impossible to shut out and Ray knew that before long tempers would become frayed and nerves would be stretched to breaking point.

Emma Thorn and two others had been talking quietly together on the opposite side of the room. Emma spoke for them.

'Why the change in pattern? As you said, Lee was discreet. Self-contained almost. This one seems to need to advertise. It's as though he's saying, "Look at me. You can puzzle all you like, try every way of looking at this, and you still won't understand me." '

'That's pretty much what the profilers have come up with,' Beckett said. 'They believe that this man sees himself as invulnerable. We can't catch him. Lee didn't see himself that way.'

'Lee knew he would be caught,' Ray said quietly. 'He didn't care. His only concern was that he completed the ritual. And when he failed, he still kept that wish alive. Whoever it was must have known Lee and what he was doing, and, according to the beliefs of the cult, waiting for his death as a signal to begin again was quite logical. Lee would be free to supervise, no longer locked away in prison, which means our main suspects have to be among those who were in the cult eleven years ago. Bryn and Irene included, I suppose. Quite a few of Farrant's lot. Others probably that we don't know about.' He moved over to where the photographs of Simon's bedroom had been pinned to a board. 'This is more than exhibitionism. It's triumphal. To me, he's saying, "I have the last piece of the puzzle and you can't stop me carrying things to their conclusion." This man is gloating.'

'And if he needs Katie?'

Ray frowned. 'I think he already has Katie,' he said.

'I think we – I – gave her to him that day out at the chapterhouse.'

'But if you're right and the motorcyclist is the boy who saved her life, how does that fit in with him possibly killing her now?' Emma argued.

'It makes perfect sense in a way,' Beckett said, following the train of Ray's thought. 'Lee failed and those who knew what he was trying to do either chose to die or were killed. Probably by Morgan. Maybe he was in on it and didn't want to be implicated. Maybe he truly was appalled by what Lee had done and convinced his associates that they deserved to die. Frankly, I'm keeping an open mind on that. The boy, maybe he had his own reasons for wanting Lee to succeed. I don't know.'

'Sounds complex,' someone commented. 'I don't get all this religious stuff. Give me a straightforward domestic any day.'

There was a ripple of grim laughter. Domestics were never straightforward and no one liked playing peacemaker between warring partners.

'Why did Katie go with him?' Beckett questioned.

'Impulse,' Ray said. 'I don't believe she thought it through, but I do believe that something about the man told her that he and the boy who had saved her life were the same person. He'd saved her once, he'd been there. I don't think she'd any option but to go with him, not having come so far. He had the answers she was looking for, including, I think, the most important one.'

'Which is?'

'I think Katie wants to know who she is,' Ray said.

'She loves her foster family and thinks of them as Mum and Dad, but even the most contented of kids still need to find their roots.'

'And we've no clue?'

'We don't even have complete lists for eleven years ago. Members came and went. A hard core stayed, but even the lists of permanent members are sketchy and there's evidence that many of the records were destroyed. Most of what we knew about those living at the original house came from two old ladies who lived just down the road. They're both dead now and even then their memories were a little unreliable. They got the new inhabitants mixed up with the original family.'

'One more thing I don't get,' Beckett said. 'If Bryn and Irene out at Sommers House are right and Lee believed that he was ushering in some new messiah, why was there no claimant?'

'Would you want to admit that three children had been killed because of you?'

'No, I wasn't thinking that. It's more that I would have expected someone to point the finger.'

'Maybe anyone who knew for certain was already dead. Maybe the claimant was dead. If Morgan was out for vengeance, or justice, or simply wanted to cover his arse, you'd have assumed the claimant would have been among the first of his targets.'

Beckett nodded. 'Maybe. We've had people interviewing the New Vision lot, but they're about as much help as a lorryload of monkeys. They know nothing. They want to forget Lee and all he stood for. They talk about Morgan as some sort of martyr who died to cleanse the group of its impurities and they don't have a good word to say for Martyn Shaw. Beyond that, well . . . I'd like to see their faces if we prove that Morgan didn't die that night.'

'Have you had anyone else go out to Sommers House?'

'Two of the locals went on our behalf, just to check things out. That was earlier this morning. Reckon they were made welcome and that the kids climbed all over them, wanting to play with the handcuffs.' He smiled. 'I think they went in there expecting to see pictures of Satan on the walls and pentacles drawn on the floors in virgin's blood, not to be offered tea and cake.'

Ray nodded. 'I'm wondering if we've played this wrong,' he said. 'I thought I was giving them good advice, but I'm not so sure now.'

'What are you thinking? That we should let the media into Sommers House?'

'It might be a way of defusing some of the tension,' Ray said.

'You think the Sommers lot would agree to it?'

'I don't know, but I think it's worth talking about. Once there's no mystery, some of the pressure might come off.'

'And it could backfire painfully, depending on the tone of the reporting. The public don't want to read that Sommers is as innocent as a convent. Listen to them out there. They want justice and they want blood, and if we don't put an end to this soon I don't think they'll be too particular whose blood they get.'

Chapter Twenty-Seven

Katie had been alone all day and when Nathan returned she was so relieved to have company that she forgot to be afraid of him.

'Where have you been? I thought they must have caught you.'

'Would you care?' he asked. 'Or would you just be afraid that no one would find you?'

'Would you tell them?' Katie asked anxiously. 'If you were arrested, would you tell them I was here?'

'Arrested for what?'

She shrugged. 'You know.'

He said nothing and as she blinked he had shifted across the room, slipping off his jacket. He went into the little kitchen and began to prepare food for them both. Katie had begun to realize that much of the food he brought home was for her. He ate little, merely picking at his plate.

She followed him into the kitchen and took up position beside the door. 'What are you?' she asked again.

He hesitated, his gaze wandering back out into the curiously decorated basement. 'I don't know,' he said softly. His eyes finally came to rest upon her face and she was struck by how rarely he chose to look right at her. When he did it was almost painfully intense.

'He made me into something else,' Nathan said. 'But

what he did wasn't complete. While he was locked away like that he couldn't finish it. Now he's dead in this life and he's sent his soul out to finish what he started. Finish making me into that other thing. He said I was an avatar. Like a messiah. The link between mankind and the angels. He said that it was a kind of evolution and that one day we would all be like this. The way he said that I was meant to be. But he and Daniel Morgan argued. Morgan said that I wasn't right, that I wasn't pure enough, but Harry Lee went ahead anyway. He said that Morgan was wrong and finally Morgan agreed with him. I think Morgan had tried something like this already, but Lee said that he had failed.'

He hesitated again and then he led her back through to the main room and stood her beside the makeshift altar.

'Seven is a sacred number. The number of movement and transformation. Three boys then and three boys now, that makes six.'

'And the seventh?'

Katie thought she could guess the answer.

Chapter Twenty-Eight

Bryn, Irene and the others sat in the meeting room and listened to Irene talking about her dream. During the day she had thought about it a great deal and sought interpretation, and she had now become convinced that the dream was a message and that the young man represented the one chosen by Lee to be his successor. That through this man, Lee was committing the murders.

'You think that he's a real person?' Mitch asked. 'Why not some kind of archetype? That makes more sense. The embodiment of your fear and ours. It doesn't follow that he's a real individual.'

'I know it's hard for you,' Amy said to Irene. 'That for those of us who were around then this has a personal side to it. But Irene, we had nothing to do with Lee killing then and we have nothing to do with what is happening now. Lee was insane. I agree with Mitch that you're dreaming because you're afraid, not because you're receiving messages. You know what the Prophet tells us, that we should look for all logical explanations first. Only when we've sifted through those can we accept that there might be something else.'

'And even then, the Prophet tells us it only seems supernatural because we don't yet know the mechanics,' Mitch added.

'I know that,' Irene said impatiently, 'but Lee sent his soul.'

'Maybe he did,' Mitch said gently. 'But equally, maybe this is someone jumping on the bandwagon. Lots of murderers have copycats. But even if he did and you're right, all the more reason to distance ourselves. Whatever community Lee had been a part of, he would still have been an evil man. The Prophet told us we should start again and reject all of that. I thought that's what Sommers House was about. Making a new start, the best, most loving and positive community possible.'

Irene was clearly not convinced, though the murmurs from the rest of the community told Mitch that they agreed with her. Most of them were young, had been children or teenagers when Lee had broken the first community. They had come here to join the Eyes of God as it now was and loved their home at Sommers. They didn't want all of this dragged up again. Their families were worried about them already and the effect that all of this was having on the children was exactly what they had come to Sommers to avoid.

There was clearly something else on Irene's mind and it occurred to Mitch that Bryn had been unusually silent throughout the session. She was about to speak to him when Irene began to talk again.

'I was very close to Morgan, you all know that. When we began to suspect what Lee might be doing he said that we must all atone for it.'

'That's enough,' Bryn snapped uncharacteristically. Usually he was the most softly spoken and patient of men.

Mitch looked at them both, aware that everyone in the room shared her puzzlement.

'He and the others killed themselves because of Lee?' asked Mitch. 'I know there were rumours, Irene, but surely . . .'

'I heard,' someone else commented, 'that other arrests might have been made. Accomplices of Lee's. Is that true?'

Bryn got to his feet and crossed to the heavily curtained window. He lifted the drape aside, just a fraction, and peered out before letting it fall. He shook his head.

'Lee acted alone,' he said, 'but there were others of us who suspected, right from the outset. Maybe we could have stopped things.'

'And you did nothing?' Mitch had not meant to sound so shocked.

'It wasn't like that,' he said with a touch of asperity. 'Irene and I, we knew that Lee believed in the power of a particular ritual. I don't know where he got the idea from, it certainly wasn't part of the original teachings, and, though Lee talked about it as a kind of alchemy, all the talk of the purifying power of fire and the transformation of the alembic, nothing I have read in the literature was exactly like he envisaged. Morgan argued with him for a while, but Harry was very persuasive and after a while . . . I think even Morgan gave in to it.

'Lee wanted to bring in what he saw as a new age. Summon the new avatar. We all thought he'd gone crazy, but there were others willing to follow him. Morgan was not so careful of his membership as Martyn has been. There were those who had fled to us because they could not cope with the real world. The thought of tearing down reality and rebuilding something mystical was what appealed to them. The powerless craved power, even though they couldn't even handle what went on in the everyday world. They thought they could wield and control the kind of pseudo-magic that Lee was selling them.'

'Bryn and I, we went to Morgan,' Irene went on. 'He told us not to worry, that he could calm things down and make Harry Lee see the error of his ways.' She laughed harshly. 'We didn't know that by that time Morgan believed in everything that Harry was doing. We'd gone to him for help, not knowing that he'd become a part of the problem.'

'But why kill the children? I don't understand that,' Mitch said.

Irene looked uncomfortable. 'Innocent blood,' she said. 'They were, he said, old enough to feel the first stirrings of adolescence but not to have done anything about it. "The fire has been kindled in the blood, but does not yet burn too bright." Those were his words, Mitch, but we didn't understand what he meant. Not until afterwards. He took the blood, purified it, transformed it. The little girl, I don't really understand why he needed her, she was far too young . . .' Colour rose to her cheeks and she looked away.

'You think that Morgan . . . or Lee . . . Irene, are you telling me Lee considered raping this child before he murdered her?'

'No! Of course not,' Irene protested, but her expression told Mitch that she suspected that very thing.

165

'The mystic sister,' Bryn said softly. 'The bringing together of male and female, fire and water, all of the elements.'

Mitch shook her head. 'Alchemical teaching is about a meeting of equals, Bryn. Not about the rape and murder of little children. It's about the purity of the individual soul, not the making of some . . . monster.' She shook her head angrily. 'You knew all this?' she demanded. 'You knew all about this, suspected what might be going on, and you said nothing? Three children died, and now at least two more. Irene, why didn't you go straight to the police?'

'This was not a matter for the police,' Irene told her angrily. 'It's a matter for our consciences. We did what we believed was right at the time. We weren't to know that Morgan had lost his mind.'

'No. No, it's not,' Mitch protested. 'This has nothing to do with conscience, religious or otherwise. Irene, we're talking about murder. The killing of little children.'

Bryn and Irene looked at one another, their faces full of pain. It was clear from the shocked silence in the room that most of the others agreed with Mitch and could not believe that they had stood by and done nothing.

'And you were supposed to die that night, weren't you?' Mitch asked softly. 'You're telling me that at the last minute Morgan stopped believing in Lee and got an attack of conscience. Decided you and he and all those other people should die to pay for those kids' lives?'

'He didn't die,' Irene whispered, so quietly that at first Mitch wasn't sure she'd heard her right. 'We escaped, and so did Morgan. We were supposed to go back to the

Markham house that night, but my mother had just died and I couldn't go. Bryn stayed with me. We saw Morgan later and he said that he was glad we'd got away. That he knew we could be trusted to say nothing and that one day he'd be back and need people loyal to him. To be ready for him. Only those most faithful to Lee were at the house that night. Fire cleanses, Mitch. They knew what they were doing.' She shook her head. 'I don't know if I would have gone anyway. I believed in Morgan and his teachings, I was never so certain about Lee.'

'And what about Martyn?' Mitch asked desperately. 'Surely he wasn't mixed up in all of this?'

Irene closed her eyes and shook her head. 'Martyn was away, studying. He'd been kept right out of all this deliberately. Morgan wanted him unsullied by it. But Martyn knew that something was wrong. All that day he had tried to reach us, but Morgan had disconnected the phones and told us all to stay inside. By the time Martyn decided that he had to come and find out what was wrong, it was all too late. He turned up at the house in the early hours of the morning, right in the middle of the investigation. The fire service was still damping down and Katie had been taken away. The rest was gone.'

'And does Martyn know about all this? That you and Morgan and Lee . . .'

'I don't know what Martyn does or does not know,' she said. 'We hardly saw him back then and he was never told that we should have died. He's accepted us, always, as loyal members of the new organization and we've worked hard for him.'

'And Morgan. How do you feel about him?'

'We owe him nothing,' Bryn told her. 'He abandoned us. Lied to us. We have no wish to have him back, not now.'

'Have you thought it might be Morgan who's been killing those children?' Mitch questioned, aware that her voice had grown shrill with the panic and outrage she was feeling. 'You've got to tell the police.'

Again, Irene and Bryn exchanged a glance. 'In the morning,' Irene promised. 'Give us this night, Mitch. In the morning we'll call your friend and tell the police everything we know.'

Mitch stared at them for a moment and then left the meeting room. Behind her she could hear the arguments continuing and then, as she reached her bedroom door, others spilling out into the hall. Some were crying, unable to believe that the couple they had seen as their leaders for so long could have been so mistaken in their actions.

Mitch went into her room and locked the door. She hesitated only for a moment more, then she rummaged in the bedside drawer for her mobile and called George.

Chapter Twenty-Nine

George was at his London home when he took the call. It took several minutes for him to sort out what it was that had upset Mitch so much.

'It's going to take me a good couple of hours to reach you,' he told her, 'even at this time of night. I'll call Ray and get him to come out to you. He'd better notify Beckett as well.'

'I can't believe they knew and did nothing,' Mitch ranted. Later, she would cry, but just now all she could feel were outrage and anger.

'It might not have been as clear-cut as that,' George said, trying to soothe her.

'You weren't there. You didn't hear what they had to say.'

'No, but I will be soon, Mitch, I will be soon. Now let me call Ray and I'll be with you as quickly as I can.'

Ray was at Sarah's but neither of them was asleep. Sarah insisted that she wanted to go along too. They paused only long enough to get dressed and inform Beckett of developments. He promised to phone ahead and tell the local officers that they'd be coming through the cordon.

'Let me know when you get there and if you need back-up.'

'I will. It might amount to nothing, of course. George says that Mitch was close to hysterical.'

'Well, check it out anyway. But, Ray, if they have information and they've been withholding it, believe me, I'll see they burn.'

'Do you know who I am?' Katie asked Nathan. 'Who my parents were?'

He shook his head. 'Not really. Your mother was there, I think. I don't think your father belonged to us. I saw you with a woman, she was crying, trying to get you to drink your juice. You didn't like it.'

'My mother gave it to me?' Katie was shocked. Somehow she had always had a picture of her mother knowing nothing. Of maybe being stolen from home and her parents never knowing what became of her. It had never occurred to her that her parents might have had a role in this. 'Maybe she wasn't my mother,' she told him angrily.

Nathan shrugged. 'Maybe,' he said. But she knew that he didn't believe that.

'What about your parents? Were they there?'

'My mother was in love with Lee.'

'And, was Lee your . . .'

He nodded. 'I think so.'

'And did she die?'

'She liked orange juice,' he told her simply.

He got up and began to pace restlessly about the room, pausing now and then to examine one of the images painted on the wall. Katie watched him, her mind still

170

reeling from the shock of the details he had just revealed. She didn't want to cry, worried that if she started she wouldn't be able to stop, but in the end she gave in and allowed fat tears to roll down her cheeks. The half-memory of a young blonde woman bending down to pick her up sprang into her mind. The woman she had dreamed about so many times, that must be her mother, the woman who'd been willing to let her die. Willing and compliant.

'I was twelve years old,' Nathan said suddenly. He was standing in front of her. She could see his legs through a haze of tears, and his voice came from far above her head.

'Did you see him kill the boys?' Her voice sounded fuzzy, thick with tears, and she sniffed loudly, trying to keep her nose from running.

'I saw them die,' Nathan said. 'He made me watch. He made me do other things too, said the alchemy must work a certain way. And now it's begun again and you're the last, Katie.' He knelt down and leaned forward, kissing her lightly on her forehead.

Chapter Thirty

Ray was momentarily blinded by a dozen camera flashes as they drove through the cordon at Sommers House. Their arrival, he thought, was probably the most interesting thing that had happened there in days.

Mitch must have been watching for them, because the front door opened as soon as the car pulled up on the gravel drive. She threw herself into Ray's arms, then pulled back with a murmured apology.

'Come on,' Ray said gently, taking her arm. 'Let's go inside.'

Their arrival had disturbed the others. No one had been sleeping, except the children, though most of the adults had retreated to their rooms after the meeting.

'What's going on, Mitch?'

'You *phoned* these people? After Bryn and Irene asked you to wait?'

'What choice did she have? We should have insisted, not just sat around looking at one another, wondering what to do.'

Ray half listened to the protests as he led Mitch through to the kitchen. 'Where *are* Bryn and Irene?' he asked, glancing around. Most of the adults had crowded behind them into the kitchen. He had expected Bryn and Irene to be the first there, asking questions, outraged at this lack of protocol.

People looked at one another, glances showing that they too wondered what had happened to the community leaders.

'We left them in the meeting room,' Amy said.

'If they were still there, they'd have heard the noise. It's only across the hall.'

'They wouldn't come out if they were meditating.'

But it didn't feel that simple.

Mitch went back into the hall, the others following. She tried the door to the meeting room and found it locked. They knocked, called out, but no one replied.

The spare keys were in the dining room and Mitch ran to fetch them. The door was opened.

Bryn and Irene lay on the floor close to the altar wall. Both were dead.

Chapter Thirty-One

When George arrived Ray filled him in quickly. It wasn't yet clear how Bryn and Irene had died, but their bodies had lost little heat and preliminary time of death was put at around midnight.

'Mitch called you at eleven-thirty. Then you called me and we left Sarah's just after twelve. Mitch thinks that if she'd known, she could have called an ambulance but she was already in her room and didn't come back down. She's blaming herself for not realizing what they were planning when they asked her to wait until morning.'

A family – husband, wife, two sleepy children – came downstairs carrying suitcases.

'What's happening?' George asked.

'There are chapterhouses in Scotland and in Wales. Those with kids have asked to leave once they've given statements. The locals can take over from there and social services are being briefed. It seems the best way, getting the kids out of here. Beckett's asked for the locals to escort them and block the roads to stop the press from following. That's being done.'

George nodded. 'Where's Mitch?' he asked.

'Dining room. Sarah's with her.'

*

Mitch was sitting in the corner with Sarah beside her. She looked pale and tired and had obviously been crying for a long time, her eyes reddened and her cheeks blotched and stained. A WPC sat on her other side, going through her statement and trying to add detail, though Mitch was clearly finding it hard to make sense.

George hugged her and shook her gently, then told her sternly to pull herself together. The WPC looked outraged, but it seemed to work. She even managed a watery smile. He then wandered off to talk to DI Winters, the local officer in charge, who seemed to be expecting him. Following behind, Ray heard part of the exchange.

'Beckett spoke to me about you,' Winters said, 'and then my boss got a call from some bloke called Dignan. Home Office apparently. We've been asked to extend you every courtesy, whatever that might mean.'

He clearly resented this trampling on his turf. A retired police officer on the scene he could just about handle, provided he respected protocol and kept out of the way. George was a different matter.

'I'd just like access to a telephone,' George reassured him, 'and I'd like to take my young friend home when she's given her statement. I do hope that's all right.'

Sarah called to Ray at that point and he heard no more of their conversation. She stood in the kitchen door with yet another tray of tea for him to distribute. George sauntered over to join him as he was handing it out.

'Thought you'd retired,' Ray said sarcastically. 'And since when has Dignan been Home Office?'

'It's strictly true, in one sense,' George told him comfortably. 'They pay him a small retainer. I thought a call from him might smooth our way. Where were the bodies found, Ray?'

Ray took him through to the meeting room. The bodies were being bagged ready for removal. George's gaze took in the paintings on the wall, depictions of men and falling angels.

'They have a perfect alibi for the murders,' Ray commented softly. 'All of them, being here, under the direct gaze of a couple of dozen journalists. Had they not, then things would have been quite different once Beckett heard about that.'

He pointed at the altar wall and the flowing gold-edged script that read, 'Man is like an angel falling.'

'You've got to talk to Martyn Shaw,' Ray told Mitch when she had finished giving her statement. 'He'll have been told by now, but he'll want to talk to someone on the scene. Someone he knows.'

Mitch nodded. 'We'll use the video phone,' she said.

The media room was an eye-opener. Ray had no idea what most of the equipment did, he was only just getting used to computers. George, however, seemed right at home, taking over from Mitch when she seemed unequal to the task of even dialling the code.

They got through to Chicago, where it was late evening. When Martyn's image appeared it was against a backdrop of blue-black sky and glassy lake.

'Mitch! My God, I'm so sorry. Are you all right? The children . . .'

Mitch collapsed once more into sobs and George took over, introducing himself briefly.

'Mitch told me about you,' Martyn said. 'She told me that you're a good friend. But is everyone else all right? All I know is that Bryn and Irene killed themselves.'

He was visibly shaken, clearly distressed. George did not trouble to mince his words.

'You care about these people?'

'You know I do.'

'Then get here now. I'll make the arrangements and call you back in, say, an hour. We'll organize a quiet entry for you and a safe house. Then you can tell us what the hell is going on.'

Ray expected Shaw to protest, but he simply nodded. 'I'll be packed and ready to leave,' he said.

Chapter Thirty-Two

They had returned to Sarah's cottage and an exhausted Mitch been installed in Sarah's bed. It was getting on for six o'clock by the time George left them and headed back to London to finalize arrangements for Martyn Shaw. He was very tired but would not give in to Sarah's urgings to at least have a couple of hours sleep before he went. Sarah herself had decided to phone in sick later on. She had the feeling that it was not only Ray who had been caught on camera the night before and really couldn't face the explanations should her colleagues see her on the morning news.

'It's a mess,' she commented as they sat in her small kitchen, looking out over the fields and watching the sky lighten with the promise of dawn.

'I don't think we know the half of it yet,' Ray said. He had called Beckett and brought him up to speed. Asked about the boy, but there was nothing new.

Sarah had a portable television in the kitchen and she switched it on. They watched the early-morning news. The media already carried new pictures of Sommers House, the police cordon and one of the families leaving, escorted by police motorcyclists. Sketchy reports were emerging, rumours of murder or suicide, though as yet there had been no official statement.

Speculation grew on the back of speculation. Experts

were trundled on to give their views. In the absence of fact, comparisons were being made with Waco and Jonestown and the Church for the Restoration of the Ten Commandments in Uganda. Comparisons that were as inappropriate as they were grotesque.

Ray tolerated it until he heard a psychologist talking about the children, speculating about the effects that these events might have on them. There were vague hints about abuse and satanic cults, nothing concrete but enough to start rumours. Even though Ray knew they were quite unfounded, he could well understand how such stories could grow, especially bearing in mind how suspicious and strange the Eyes of God must seem to the outside world.

He switched channels, only to find Farrant and New Vision taking up space there. Farrant looked almost gleeful as the presenter asked him to comment on the reports coming out of Sommers. The same film was shown, families leaving, police escort. The road block to prevent pursuit. The same rumours of death.

'I wish that I could say I'm surprised,' Farrant intoned. 'But I'm not. There has always been a history of mental instability among the membership and the leaders of the Sommers community were known associates of Harrison Lee. All I can say is that these events are tragic. We must all learn from them and hope that the children will receive proper counselling.'

Ray turned off in disgust.

He was worn out and so was Sarah. They fetched spare blankets and made up the bed-settee in the living room, falling asleep within minutes.

Chapter Thirty-Three

Nate remembered what it had been like. The boy in the cellar, knowing that he was going to die.

'What's your name?' he had asked.

'Nathan. Please, can you get me out of here? I'm scared.'

'I don't know.' Nate had looked around at the basement decorated with the images of man and falling angels, at the tiny barred window through which, at sunset, the sky cast fire onto the tiled floor and the massive oak door that led back into the rest of the house.

'I'll try,' he promised, looking into the dark eyes of the young boy who knelt in the darkened corner, his hands bound behind his back and his dirty face streaked by his tears.

The others had not woken up. They had stayed sleeping while Harry did all of those things he said he had to do. While he had made Nate watch and sometimes do things too, at what he said were the proper times in the rite.

But Harry had delayed the killing this time for reasons that Nate could not understand and Harry had delayed too in giving the other one the stuff he needed that made him feel good. In control.

The boy had begun to cry again, his face crumpling and his soft dark eyes filling up with tears.

'I'll try and get help,' Nate said. 'Get to a phone.' Yes, that was it, though even as he thought it the words lost cohesion and slid from his mind, like the boy's tears, slipping to the floor.

And then the other one was there, the other angel with them in the room. The one that Harry and Morgan argued over, fought to replace him with. Nate remembered that he ran over to the boy and began to untie his hands. 'Help me,' he commanded. 'Help me get him out of here.' But the other one just shook his head and Nate knew that he was right. It was impossible. They were as trapped, as unable to run, as Nathan himself.

'There was another angel,' Nathan told Katie. 'Morgan and Harry Lee argued over which one of us was most righteous. The other one . . . something happened to him. He started to act strangely. Lee and Daniel Morgan gave him drugs, I think, and then one day he simply wasn't around any more. After that they concentrated on me, but they still argued about us and sometimes . . . sometimes it was almost like they couldn't decide which of us was real.'

He fell silent for a little while and Katie, getting wise to his moods now, waited patiently. Finally he began to speak again, his body still and tense and his gaze unfocused, as though he was watching something far away.

'I watched the places where I knew he'd leave them. I knew he'd follow the pattern like last time, but I was wrong. He'd sacrificed the ritual so that he could let me know that he was as aware of me as I was of him. He brought the body here and left it outside my door, like a cat bringing in a mouse and expecting praise. I couldn't have that, Katie. I couldn't have him bringing the bodies to me. It was all wrong. So I took the boy and I laid him out where Lee left the first one. And I covered him up, tried to keep him safe.'

'Who is it?' Katie asked again.

'He's like me. He's older and stronger, but he's just like me. He slips through the shadows and he disappears into the sunlight and I can feel him. I know the way he thinks and when I moved the body it was like starting a conversation with him. Like we were performing in the same play.'

Chapter Thirty-Four

Ray and Sarah woke to the sound of the telephone and Ray knew intuitively that it would be Beckett.

'They've found Simon Ellis,' he told Sarah as he replaced the receiver. 'He was lying at the foot of the cellar steps in the Robin on the Green.'

'You'll be going now then?'

Ray nodded. 'I don't know how I feel,' he said. 'It's all wrong, I know, but I'm almost relieved. That's the three of them. At least there'll be no more.'

He met Sarah's frank gaze, knowing that she would understand what he was saying and not judge him for it.

'What about Katie?' she asked softly, and Ray felt the knot tighten once more at the pit of his stomach.

Nate remembered how he had untied the boy's hands and was helping him to his feet. The boy was gazing at him with a look caught between terror and admiration. He started to speak, but Nate hushed him and led him forward, his feet stumbling a little from the effects of the drug and immobility.

'We have to be quiet, really quiet.' He glanced back at the other one, the older boy who seemed to live in a world that no one else shared, and he hoped that this other angel would understand enough not to shout or make a fuss when they left.

He had Nathan by the hand and pulled him forward towards the big door. He held him back for a moment as he pulled the handle and the door swung inward, surprisingly light and balanced despite its mass. He wasn't sure how they would get through the house. Hopefully there would be no one in the kitchen and they could get out through there without being seen. He didn't even know if the others were in on this act of Lee's. Harry Lee had sworn him to secrecy and told him that if he spoke about any of it, he would end up as dead as the boys. He believed what Lee said. The man was so single-minded, so obsessed, he let nothing get between him and his goal. He didn't know these others but had to assume they were the same. All he wanted now was for this to end. To get out with Nathan and then run as far and as fast as he could. He hadn't given any thought to where.

But they didn't even make it to the top of the basement stairs. Harry Lee himself stood there, the height and weight of him filling the narrow doorway and blocking off the light.

'Harry!'

Lee didn't even look at him. He reached out, grabbed the boy Nathan by the throat and flung him back down the cellar stairs, smashing his face against the wooden door.

'I want to keep you safe,' Nathan said. 'I brought you here so you'd be away from him.'

Katie shook her head. 'You can't. Not this time, this is different.'

'I kept you safe before. Morgan said I should wait until the others were sleeping, then bring you out. He meant for you to die that night. He knew that Harry Lee had been arrested and wanted to complete the ritual before the police came. He knew they would, eventually, when they found out who Harry was and what he belonged to. No one had heard about the Eyes of God before then. We were nothing until Harry Lee.

'He told me to stop you drinking the juice, quietly, so no one else would notice. Just make up some reason to get you away from the rest and bring you out when he fetched the car round. I hid you. I was going to tell him that you must have run away. I figured you'd be safe where I left you and if you hadn't drunk the juice then you'd be all right.

'Then I heard the sirens and I heard Morgan's car drive away really fast. Without me. And I ran outside, ran up the road after him, and I could hear the sirens in the distance. It was such a still, cold night. The moon had a frost ring all around it and there were stars everywhere, shining down and sparkling through the frost. I must have chased a mile down the road after Morgan's car and I realized that the sirens were getting closer. They would have been right up on the main road when I first heard them and the sound carried in the night, it was so still and so clear.' He turned to look at her. 'I remembered that, the other day when I came for you. Sound wouldn't carry so far in the day, not with the rain and all the damp trees, but I remembered how the sound had travelled that

185

night and I cut the engine, pushed the bike the final mile. I watched you all, poking around in the grass, trying to get it figured out.'

'Did you call the police?'

Nathan nodded. 'Should have done it before,' he mumbled. 'But I knew he'd kill me. Then when Morgan said Lee'd been arrested, I knew I had to try and do something. I didn't know he'd rigged the place to explode. I just thought the juice would kill everyone. I heard the explosion as I turned to go back. I'd never heard anything like that. It was so angry, so loud, and the ground shook even though I'd run so far away. I picked myself up and walked back. I thought you must be dead. That what I'd tried to do hadn't helped. By the time I got back to the Markham house the police were all over it and everyone else was gone.'

'What did you do?'

'I hid.'

The emergency services had set up dragon light all around the house, but beyond the circle of light the darkness had been intense. He had watched and waited. Seen the others arrive. Bryant, Ray Flowers and his team. Seen the old man die and Katie lifted from the ruins. And he had known that at least he had done one thing right.

'Later, I saw Martyn Shaw arrive. It was close to dawn by then and he drove up in his big old estate car, drove right past me, and when he got out of the car he left the door open and I climbed inside and hid under a blanket in the boot space. I hid there until he drove away.'

'Martyn Shaw knew?'

Nathan shook his head. 'No. I told him later. He knew nothing before. Morgan kept him away at university. Said he had to study and finish his education before he decided what to do finally. He knew that Martyn would never agree, but he thought that once everything was done, the Prophet would have nothing he could argue about. The avatar would be here and no one could undo it. Martyn suspected something, he kept getting visions of fire and death and someone running away, but he didn't know what it was and didn't want to believe it was as bad as it felt. Morgan had been so important to him. Understood him when no one else had.'

Katie frowned. 'We can't do this on our own. I'm scared.'

'He can't get in here.'

'No? What's stopping him?' She waved a hand, encompassing the room in her gesture. 'This magic? I want to see my mum and dad.'

The look he gave her told her that he didn't understand. Nathan, she was learning, lived by his own rules, played life as some complex game she didn't begin to understand. She had an awful suspicion there was only one other in the universe who would, and that one killed children.

'I'll take a letter to your parents,' he said finally. That was the most he was prepared to do.

Ray had not bothered to ask for directions, he knew where Beckett would be. Since Ray had drawn his attention to the link with previous murders, Beckett had set a twenty-four-hour watch on the prospective locations. The second time, the real site was now a supermarket and the killer had left the body in the next-door building site. This time, Beckett told him angrily, he must have walked right past the four men on watch carrying the child's body.

'I needed more people. Look at this place. He could have come from any of half a dozen directions. I'd got road blocks on all the main roads leading here but that still doesn't cover the back alleys and cut-throughs. I've pulled in extra personnel from Leicester and Nottingham and it's not enough. What the fuck are we dealing with here?'

Ray shook his head. He remembered the same frustrations from the last time. 'I know,' he said. 'I grew up round here. You could get the length of the street going across the garden walls and through the alleyways. All the demolition's done is make it even easier.'

Beckett led him through to what had been the Robin on the Green pub yard. Ray could recall Sunday afternoons sitting here with his mum and dad. There'd been picnic benches and a bit of an area with swings for the kids to play in. Kids with their Vimto bottles and their bags of crisps, most waiting for their dads to come out of the public bar where children were banned. He'd not been back in eleven years. The wake for his mum's funeral had been held in the reception room here and it had continued to be his dad's local long after that. But his dad couldn't face it, not once the boy had been found dead, and now the pub itself had been abandoned. Boarded up and left to rot.

'There's a cellar here,' Ray mused vaguely.

'We've searched it, top to bottom.'

Ray sighed. 'Course you have. Clutching at straws. This one, the boy, it'll be different.'

Beckett nodded. 'The other two were practically unmarked. This one had the side of his face smashed, like he'd hit it on the corner of something.'

'Little Nathan Brown had a shattered cheekbone and a long bruise down his face, as though he'd smashed into a door.' He sighed heavily. 'It wasn't reported, not anywhere, about the other injury. His mum and dad might have told, of course, or the mortuary attendant, or the police officers who saw the body, or . . .'

'Any one of fifty people. No such thing as non-disclosure, is there? Just restriction. But when it's all over, people talk. You can't expect them not to. Chances are, a great many people have the wherewithal to copy this, but I agree with you, it's most likely someone who was witness to the killings last time. Though he hasn't kept to every detail. Simon's room, that was new.'

'And I still haven't figured out why. It seems excessive. Gilding the lily, so to speak. Unless he deliberately wanted the Eyes to be implicated and that was as important as the actual killing.'

'Sounds like revenge. Someone wants to make them pay for . . . what? Letting Lee down? Killing someone in the explosion? Following false prophets? . . . When does he arrive, by the way?'

'This evening. George has it all in hand.'

'So I heard. Doesn't mind what toes he treads on, does he?'

'Not so as I've noticed. All right, let's have a look then.'

He crossed somewhat reluctantly to the body, which was already prepared for removal. The boy lay swathed in a blanket, over-wrapped in a white sheet, and was packed into the black body bag. His face was bloodied and swollen. The wound had had time to bleed and bruise before he died. Ray closed his eyes and prayed silently that the child had been unconscious when the blow landed and shattered the bones of his cheek and jaw.

'And now there's only Katie,' he said.

Katie had grown tired of wearing the same clothes, feeling dirty and dishevelled, and earlier she had bathed and then washed her clothes in the bath, using shampoo to get them clean. Nathan had lent her an old shirt. It was too big for her, the sleeves coming down over her hands and the tails reaching to her knees, but she wore it now, sleeping peacefully on the cushions. He had lain down beside her, curling his body around hers. She smelt of peach shampoo. He had bought that thinking she would like it and her still-damp hair held on to the fragrance. He breathed it in as he lay there, closing his eyes until his mind was filled only with the warmth of her body and the scent of her perfume, of clean skin and peach shampoo. It was the closest Nathan had been to another person in more years than he could think. It revived memories, so ancient as to be almost sepia-toned, of someone holding him, touching him, stroking his hair and making him laugh at some long-forgotten joke. He felt confused and bereft and very scared. This, he thought – a moment of clarity breaking into the confusion – must be what her parents are feeling now, so afraid that they have lost her and that she might be gone for ever.

He waited another hour, until the evening would have closed in and darkness eaten up what little light there had been that day. Then he took Katie's letter and slipped outside, wheeling his bike back up the ramp and locking the doors tight behind him.

He delivered the letter to Ray's office rather than her parents' hotel, not certain even if the Fellowses would still be there. Ray would find it, either later that night or tomorrow morning, but they had to understand, he must keep Katie safe.

As he rode back through Mallingham he became aware of the other one. His presence on the streets, marking them with a scent that permeated everything. Nathan caught the smell of it, the familiar death smell wrapping itself around the buildings like a fog. Thicker here, lighter and more diffuse there. Bleeding through into the houses and infecting lives. He could feel the other one getting stronger, so much stronger. Could hear the voice that spoke directly into his mind, clear enough now for him almost to catch his every word.

Since that night he had kept the curtains closed and blocked out the sun. Even in the daytime, when he was forced to walk outside, he carried the shadows with him, wrapping them about himself like a cloak of dark wings.

Jane Adams

Once, when he had been really sick, he had tried to make a cloak of wings. The wings his precious moths sacrificed to him, flying into the blinding light until it scorched the life from them and they fell lightly onto the wooden floor. Sometimes so many falling that it felt like rain, the soft thud of their little bodies as they hit the floor filling him with a tainted joy.

But he had nothing with which to sew the wings, nothing to fix them, and they would not let him have needle and thread. They had no understanding, when they forced him out into the garden, into the sunlight, that all he wanted was to hide away in the dark before the light burned the life from him as it had from the sad little moths.

Later, much later, they had given him paint and he had learned to capture the images the artist had once painted on the walls. Imperfectly at first, then with more confidence as his skills grew. And he learned then that he did not need the moth wings to protect him from the sun. His mind could create its own winged shadow and he could walk in bright sun and his soul would keep from burning.

Chapter Thirty-Five

Ray had been dreaming about Katie and they had not been good dreams. He woke to the ringing of the telephone and for a moment he lay there, breathless with fear, as the ringing stopped and he heard Sarah speaking to someone and then calling for him.

She looked pale as she handed him the telephone. 'It's Beckett,' she said. 'There's been another abduction. Another boy.'

Ray stared at her in disbelief and then took the receiver from her hand. 'What the hell . . .'

'Marcus Ellwood. Eleven years old, mixed race, lives with his grandparents in Elsingham Terrace. That's the new flats out towards the A47. They put him to bed as usual last night. This morning, he wasn't there.'

'But surely . . .' Ray's voice faded. He couldn't say the words. Surely, there should only be three. Lee only killed three.

'That's what I thought. I told myself, he'd gone off with friends. He was playing some kind of trick. He was going to turn up any time now. But then I saw his room. Ray, his grandparents sleep in the next bedroom and they never heard a thing. The flat's on the ground floor, the small window had been left open, and he used that to reach in and open the main one. Came in, took the boy and took time out to make certain we'd know it was him.'

'More graffiti?'

'Last time was nothing. Look, get over here. I want you to see this, see if it rings any bells.'

Ray replaced the receiver. He was shaking, he realized, and wanted to cry, unreasonable and infantile as that might seem to be. He felt the sobs choking his lungs and twisting at his guts and he tried to force breath back into his body, but his throat seemed blocked. Sarah came to stand beside him, wrapping her arms tight around his too big, too clumsy body.

'I was so sure.' The words came out in painful gasps.

The phone rang again and Ray groaned, certain it brought more bad news. Sarah picked it up, listened, and once more proffered it to Ray. 'It's Rowena,' she said. 'You've had a letter. It's from Katie.'

Ray almost snatched the phone.

'It was here when I arrived,' Rowena told him. 'On the hall floor with the other post, but it was just a piece of folded paper, no envelope and your name on it. It was only when I opened it I realized what it was. She wrote it to her mum and dad. Says she's OK but that she can't leave yet. She says that the boy on the bike is trying to help and that he's done nothing wrong. And not to worry.'

Ray laughed harshly at the irony in Rowena's voice. 'Try not to handle it any more than you have to,' he told her. 'Put it in an envelope and I'll take it along to Beckett, get it dusted for prints.'

As he was getting ready to leave Mitch came down the stairs.

'I heard the phone,' she said.

'He's taken another one,' Ray told her. 'Eleven years old.'

'Oh, God.'

'Why has he broken the pattern, Mitch? All he's done so far is to copy Lee. Why this one?'

News had spread fast and by the time Ray got to Mallingham a crowd had gathered. A dozen officers had been employed simply to keep order and as Ray was led through the cordon a faction of the crowd surged forward to shout at him, waving placards and demanding to know what was being done. Someone remembered that he'd been on the investigation of eleven years before.

'What's he fucking here for? Couldn't get the bastard last time round.'

Ray said nothing. He kept his head down and walked swiftly through the cordon, looking back only when he had reached the door. Many of the placards concerned the Eyes of God. 'Child Killers' he read, 'Satanists' and 'Devil Worshippers'. A woman holding a placard saw him looking and yelled that they should take *their* kids away. Social services and the police should go and raid their homes. 'Get something fucking right at least,' she yelled. 'See how the bastards like that.'

Ray turned and went through the door into the apartment block. He knew that they were wrong, the crowd, their hatred misdirected and ill-informed, but he couldn't find it in his heart to blame them. When nothing seemed to be happening, and children had died. If the killer had now broken the pattern, they might well go on dying. With that feeling of helplessness came the need for someone to blame. The scapegoat mentality was deeply ingrained, Ray had long ago figured that one out.

Beckett was waiting for him in a room that had been taken apart. Covers stripped from the bed, the sheets painted with a gaudy depiction of the human eye. The walls likewise daubed with images, not just circled eyes this time but winged figures that might have been angels, might have been something else. They appeared more insect-like, their bodies squat and stylized, with enormous wings protruding from their sides. The killer had taken plenty of time, there was no sign of frenzy or panic in the painting, each image carefully completed. The difficulty in recognition coming from a lack of skill and not of time.

'They heard nothing?' Ray questioned.

Beckett shook his head. 'The grandfather sleeps with the radio on, falls asleep listening to the World Service. The grandmother is a little deaf. The killer took the boy out through the window and must have walked back down that path between the trees to the main road.'

Ray could feel Beckett's anger.

'Do you know how many people I've got assigned to this? How many have been pulled back off sick leave, been seconded, been working double shifts?'

Ray nodded. 'I can guess.'

'You saw the crowd outside.'

'Difficult to miss.' He paused. 'It's not your fault. You're doing everything you can.'

'You think that makes it all right?'

'Of course I don't.' Ray glanced shrewdly at the other man. 'They're talking about pulling you off the case?'

Beckett nodded.

'Saying you're listening too much to an old fart who should know when he's retired?'

'They didn't put it quite that way.'

'Maybe they're right. Fat lot of use I've been so far. This time or the last.'

Beckett shook his head but said nothing to contradict him. 'When does this Martyn Shaw arrive?'

'George said he'd have him here this afternoon. His boss wants a word first.'

'Politics takes priority.' Beckett shrugged. 'Would expect no less.'

'I got this,' Ray said, producing the letter from his jacket pocket. 'Arrived at the office some time in the night or very early this morning.'

Beckett read it. 'At least she's alive,' he said grimly. 'One set of parents still have a bit of hope.'

He handed the letter back inside the plastic wallet that Rowena had placed it in. 'Show it to the parents, get them to verify the handwriting, then get it over to forensics. Not that I hold out much hope. I'll let the office know it's coming in. And we'll see what this so-called Prophet's got to say for himself this afternoon.'

Ray watched him as he strode out of the door, then followed more slowly, taking a last look around the room. The meeting between Beckett and Martyn Shaw was not going to be comfortable, he thought. Beckett was not in the mood to be either conciliatory or gentle. He thought of the young man, barely more than a boy when he had so briefly met him eleven years before, and wondered how things would turn out.

Nathan had gone out just after midday to buy food. He knew as soon as he stepped out onto the main road that something was wrong, something new had happened. It had been a feeling half with him all morning, but he had done his best to ignore it. The other one had changed something but he did not know what.

It took little time to find out. People everywhere were talking about it. The fourth child that his enemy had taken. He managed to remember what food he had set out to buy and found an early edition of the local paper, the child's face staring out at him from the front page. Then he went back to Katie, so shaken that he could barely find his way.

If Lee's three killings and then the first three here made the six, then why another? There could be only one reason left. The original ritual had been abandoned. Nathan was no longer the key. No longer chosen. The new killings had not been for him, but for the other one.

Chapter Thirty-Six

Beckett and Martyn Shaw met for the first time as the lunchtime news was playing on TV. Beckett had the set on in the incident room and watched himself coming out of this last victim's flat, his refusal to comment drawing jeers and cat-calls from the crowds.

Shaw came over and stood beside him, though neither spoke. The younger man stiffened as he saw the messages written on the placards. His lips moved slightly as he read the words.

'What did you expect?' Beckett asked him bluntly.

'I don't know. Is that Ray Flowers?' Shaw asked uncertainly as the report turned back to show images from the week and Ray was seen talking to Beckett. Ray had not been scarred the last time Shaw had seen him.

'Didn't need to be a prophet to work that one out,' Beckett told him coldly.

Shaw ignored him, watching as the news item finished with a brief interview with the vocal Mr Farrant of New Vision. 'I am appalled by all of this,' Farrant declaimed, a look on his face of intense pain and equally intense disgust. 'New Vision has no connection with any of this. You should be talking to the Eyes of God. To Martyn Shaw. Ask him if he didn't foresee any of this, with his so-called powers of prophecy. Ask him if he can't look

into his crystal ball and tell you which one of his followers is killing your children. Ask him.'

Beckett reached out and killed the set. 'And did you?'
he demanded. 'Did you foresee this? Or did your second
sight somehow let you down?'

Shaw just nodded slowly, his soft brown eyes meeting
and holding Beckett's gaze. 'Of course I knew,' he said
softly. 'Anyone who knew Lee knew what would happen
once he was dead. We warned your people what would
happen. I wrote time and again to DCI Bryant. I kept in
contact with him until he threatened to take me to court
for harassment if I didn't stop. Then I wrote to his
solicitors and I warned them. The letter should be in their
files, if anyone's bothered to ask, and in case it's not I
have copies with me of all the correspondence I ever had
with Bryant and with them. They wrote back and told
me that my concern had been duly noted. That I should
have no further anxiety. Lee was locked away.' He paused
and shook his head. 'They didn't understand, Mr Beckett,
DI Beckett or whatever it is you are. It wasn't Lee whom
I was warning you about. It was Morgan's son.'

Chapter Thirty-Seven

'Farrant knew about Morgan's son. I lost touch afterwards, but I believe Farrant knew where he went and what he did. I warned Bryant, told him that I believed Morgan had brainwashed the boy, made him believe that he was some kind of messiah. An avatar was what Morgan and Lee called him. They believed that they could bring into being some kind of saviour.'

'By killing children?'

Shaw shook his head. 'I don't pretend to understand it. When I first knew Morgan, he was a good man. Kind, gentle, probably the first person I'd ever met who didn't think I was crazy. I could talk to him about the things I saw, the things I felt. He told me he believed I was some kind of medium and should think of being trained properly. When I was about sixteen, six months or so after I had met Morgan, he took me along to this spiritualist church. Morgan wasn't a spiritualist himself, but back then he had a lot of respect for the way they trained their people. They took time and care and some churches, like this one, had what they called development circles, where people who had the gift or whatever you call it could go along and practise in safety.

'It was miraculous. The room was full of people, all sorts of people. Little old ladies who saw fairies at the bottom of their gardens. Men and women who claimed

to have Amerindian guides even though they'd never been
further west than Wandsworth. Healers who practised
the laying on of hands. Oh, I've no doubt some were
delusional. Some saw only what was inside their heads,
but there were also those, like me, who predicted events,
who felt when someone was in trouble and what that
trouble was. Who' – he shrugged – 'saw visions.'

Beckett eyed him sceptically. 'All very nice,' he said.
'But how does that help us?'

'It doesn't,' Shaw apologized. 'Why should you care
what Morgan meant to me before he came well and truly
under Lee's thumb?'

'I thought Morgan was the boss of your operation.
How come he let Lee have so much control?'

'It didn't happen overnight. Morgan met and liked
Harry Lee. It was hard not to like him, believe it or not.
Harry was a born flim-flam man. Fifty years ago and he'd
have still been selling snake oil. These days I guess he
should have stuck to cars, double-glazing, insurance
instead. Somewhere along the line he caught religion and
he started selling that. Trouble was, he began to believe
his own lies. And Morgan . . . Well, he was like many so-
called seekers. Willing to believe, concerned to seem
open-minded, just in case the truth should bite him on
the behind, disguised as something he didn't recognize, so
he listened to all that Lee had to say and he swallowed it
little by little until there was no way back.

'In that final year, eighteen months, I was away a lot.
Morgan wanted me to study and he helped me pay my
way. Finding me money for books and helping out with
lodgings. My family couldn't have done it for me and I

was grateful. But each time I came back he and Lee had gone that one step more. I didn't know where they were heading but it scared me. They read all this obscure stuff about alchemy and sacrifices and how there must be rituals to purify the soul, and they got James involved. Poor stupid James. He'd only got his father. His mother had been killed in a car crash when he was nine years old and his dad was his universe. He hated it when Morgan spent more time with his students and his good causes than he did with him and to have his dad suddenly concentrating on him big-time must have seemed like a miracle.'

'But you must have suspected what they were doing. Why didn't you go to the police?'

'No. That's where you're wrong. In the six months before the explosion I'd seen nothing of Morgan. I'd quarrelled with Lee. He was on this expansionist kick. Said that we should go out and proselytize. Get new recruits and prepare them for the new messiah. I had no truck with any of that. It wasn't my way then and it isn't now. I was amazed that Morgan went along with it.

'And I was worried about James. He was sick, completely out of it half the time. I asked Morgan point blank if he'd been taking drugs and Morgan just shrugged and said, "Whatever it takes", as though it didn't matter. I left one night after we'd had an almighty row and vowed I'd never come back. Morgan cut off all financial support and wrote to me saying that I'd have no more help until I came to my senses and saw Lee for the miracle-worker he was. There's a photocopy of the letter in the folder. I sent one to Bryant afterwards as well. I kept in touch with some of the people at the Markham house and then, when Lee stopped them writing, I kept an eye on things through the old ladies who lived down the road, Franny and Clara Albert. I called them once or twice a week and they let me know what was going on as best they could.' He shook his head. 'Not that they knew much. To them, the Markham house was another place to have tea. They were old and not altogether there. I think that's why Lee continued to tolerate them as much as he did.

'One thing I did find out. More people were moving in there, people I didn't know, and some of the old crowd had moved away. I didn't know where. The night of the explosion I'd been afraid that something would happen. I don't know why, just a bad feeling that grew all day.'

'So you decided to put aside your differences and come back home,' Beckett said sarcastically.

Shaw smiled at his tone. 'Actually, no. Franny Albert called me. Said there'd been an explosion and the place was crawling with policemen. That's why I came back.'

'How old was this son of Morgan's?'

'Somewhere about seventeen. Oh, he wouldn't be among the dead, Inspector. That's my whole point, you see. Franny Albert told me that he'd gone away. She said he'd gone to a sanatorium.' He smiled. 'She was an old lady, she used old-fashioned words, but I guessed he'd gone into either rehab or hospital. And by that time Lee had found himself another candidate for conversion. That was another thing we'd quarrelled over. He'd brought a young kid to the Markham house. Said he was his son, though I never knew if that was true. His mother had come to live with them and was having an affair with

Lee. He described her as the divine mother, if you please. The boy was about fourteen, I only saw him a couple of times before the explosion, but he wasn't among the dead either. Both of the children who died were females under twelve. Lee wouldn't let us use the boy's proper name and I don't think I ever knew it. Lee just called him his angel and when Morgan's son left the Markham house, Lee decided that his angel was the one. The chosen. His new avatar.'

'And you never tried to talk to anyone about this? Never thought about what they might have been planning?'

'You'd have believed me, would you? If I'd come to you and said that these people were planning something. That I didn't know what it was, but it involved turning a fourteen-year-old boy into a new messiah. And I thought it might involve some sort of magic. You'd have acted on it, wouldn't you?'

Beckett sighed and crossed the room to look out of the window. It had begun to rain again, light drizzle from heavy, overloaded skies. 'I don't know what I would have done,' he said. 'This was before Waco, before the Heaven's Gate suicides, before anyone had heard of the Solar Temple. Before Uganda. I don't know what I would have done.'

'Probably nothing. The police and social services were still reeling from what happened in Cumbria and Orkney hadn't happened yet. Thankfully, we believe in religious freedom in this country. The Quakers started out as just another cultish group, so did the Mormons, the Seventh Day Adventists, the Jehovah's Witnesses and dozens of others. You look deep enough into any of their pasts and you'll find a fair amount of crap. That's often just the way of it. And now you can buy your New Age trappings in the nearest supermarket. You can indulge in off-the-shelf Wicca and by-the-numbers Cabbala and no one turns a hair. And, for the most part, I think that's good. It breaks down barriers. Problem is, what might once have been difficult and inaccessible, might once have involved secret groups that selected their membership and kept them at arm's length until they were sure what made them tick, no longer exercise control. The sick-minded can get power, whether you believe in the reality of it or not, as easily as the sick in body can buy paracetamol.' He paused and shook his head. 'You wouldn't have believed me. You would have done nothing.'

Beckett still did not reply. Truth was, he was uncertain in his own mind.

Shaw changed the subject, taking Beckett by surprise. 'What happened to Ray Flowers? I almost didn't recognize him.'

'He cut himself shaving,' Beckett retorted harshly. Then he shrugged. 'Someone thought he was someone else and attacked him. Burnt his hands and face with a home-made flame-thrower. He decided to retire.'

Shaw smiled. 'I can't imagine he's as good at retirement as he was being a detective.'

Beckett shook his head. 'You're right,' he said. 'He's not. But I think he could have lived without this.' He paused, considering what Shaw had told him. 'But you must have heard about the deaths. Three boys in one small town, you can't have ignored that.'

Shaw hesitated. 'I didn't ignore it,' he said. 'When I heard about the second one I felt ... I don't know, chilled. I suppose that's the best word. But I didn't connect it to Morgan and Lee. Even in my nightmares, I didn't think that they'd go through with that.'

'Go through with it? You mean they talked about murder?'

Shaw nodded slowly. 'Lee did. He talked about blood being the life-force. About the right blood charged in the right way being the most powerful force it was possible to summon. I told him he was crazy, but Morgan came up with all of these philosophical and religious precedents. He said I was taking it too seriously, that it wasn't as if they had to drain the life from anyone. A little would do and he left it at that. I never thought he'd resort to murder.'

'Never?'

Shaw hesitated. 'I didn't want to think it. By the time the boys died I'd been away for six months or so and had seen no one from the group. I'd spoken to no one. In that six months things went seriously wrong, but I didn't realize how wrong until it was far too late.'

'How convenient,' Beckett muttered.

Shaw did not rise to the bait, just shook his head sadly. 'You don't know me, Inspector, and so I'll let that pass. I wrote, I called. I tried to keep informed by contacting those not living at the Markham house. The month before the explosion I managed to talk to Bryn. He and Irene had moved away from the Markham house to be closer to Irene's mother. She had cancer and didn't have long to live. When Franny told me that they'd gone

I called them at Irene's mother's. Bryn didn't realize who was calling and once I'd got him on the line I managed to keep him talking for a few minutes. He said that everyone was very excited, that Morgan had a big party planned for a few weeks' time. That there'd been some kind of breakthrough and everyone was going to celebrate. Then he felt guilty about talking to me and said he had to go. That's all I knew. That's really all I still know. Bryn and Irene should have been there that night but Irene's mother had just died. Irene couldn't leave her father, so they stayed. And they survived.' He hesitated and then said softly, 'I'm not sure that Irene ever forgave her mother for choosing that time to die.'

Beckett regarded him thoughtfully for a moment and then he said, 'And now. Why do you believe it's Morgan's son? You just told me that Morgan changed his mind about this so-called chosen one. That he found some other boy. Why not him?'

Shaw was shaking his head vehemently. 'No,' he said. 'It isn't him. Lee's angel hated what was going on. He hates it now.'

Beckett stiffened. 'What exactly are you telling me?' he said.

'That I've had contact with the boy since the night they all died. It isn't him.'

'Contact? What kind of contact? You didn't think to mention this to anyone?'

In reply Shaw pulled the folder he'd brought with him across the table and extracted several sheets of paper.

'Bryant knew. Bryant spoke to him. Bryant was kept informed all the way, but once he'd arrested Lee and closed the case he wouldn't listen any more. He'd had enough. He was sick and tired, he told me. Physically sick and genuinely exhausted. He had a heart condition and I understand that's what finally killed him.' Martyn Shaw sighed and then shoved the papers across the desk to Beckett. 'He promised to pass the information on and for all I know he did. Maybe it's filed away somewhere in that archive of yours, I don't know. But I did all I could to warn your people of this. I could have done nothing more.'

'And this boy, Lee's angel as you call him, where is he now?'

Martyn Shaw did not know. 'I've not spoken to him or known exactly where he is in over three years,' he said. 'He's an adult now, he goes his own way.'

'And how does he live? Does he work, draw dole, have friends? Family?'

'No, there is no one. He's had a problem forming relationships. After what happened with Lee, he finds it hard to trust anyone.'

'Except you?'

'I doubt he even trusts me. Not really. I helped him, but Lee's angel is like . . . something wild. It's like trying to define smoke, pin it down. As to how he lives, I give him money, transfer it into his account. He draws what he needs.'

Beckett pushed a pad and paper across to Shaw. 'Account number,' he said. 'Bank details, method of transfer.'

'So you can do what? Freeze the account? Trace the withdrawals?'

'Got it in one.'

Martyn shook his head. 'It's a US account,' he said. 'Transferred through a Swiss trading company. You can't have access, I'm afraid, not without a warrant from all three states. I'd guess you'd need to involve Interpol and I have no intention of giving you any details.'

He spoke with a quiet confidence and Beckett felt his pent-up anger flare. He leaned across the desk, only just preventing himself from taking the Prophet by the throat and squeezing hard.

'Three kids have died, maybe four by now, and you're trying to protect the man who might have done it. You disgust me. You make me want to puke. I could have you arrested for obstruction. I could have you hauled up in court tomorrow morning and your face splashed right across every national paper in the country. Every news bulletin. I could hold a press conference and tell the world that you have information that could lead me to the killer and you're choosing to withhold it. I could . . .'

'And you won't, Inspector. You won't do those things because innocent people would be dragged in. You accuse me, you accuse my people and you're already convinced that most if not all of them are innocent. And they too have children. I don't believe that you'll forget that. You won't do it because you know that you can't prove a thing about Lee's angel and you'd look like shit if it were proved that you'd chosen to persecute an innocent man. Someone who'd already been traumatized enough, had his entire life ripped apart by the unscrupulous bastard that killed the first three boys. You won't do it because something tells you that I'm right and he's not the one who killed those children and, most of all, you'll do nothing that could make the public aware that the police had been warned – over and over again – that this would happen once Lee was dead. That Bryant knew and held his tongue.' Shaw leaned forward, matching Beckett's gesture and body language. 'Lee scared the life from him, Beckett, both ways. When Bryant arrested him Lee cursed him. Did you know that? At first Bryant shook it off and chose to laugh about it. He was a tough old bird was Bryant, but Lee told him, first your wife will die and then your child and then, when I'm gone, I'll come for you. Six months later his wife dropped dead. Inside a year his son was killed in a hit-and-run accident; no one was ever charged. And I'll make a bet that the night he died Bryant saw something and claimed that it was Lee.'

'And how do you know all this, Mr Shaw?'

'It's in the reports, Beckett. It's all in Lee's statement. And I know because Ray Flowers told me.'

'Ray told you?'

Shaw nodded and leaned back in his chair, the tension draining from his body. He looked very tired. 'Bryant suffered from nightmares. My letters to him, my phone calls, they did nothing to help. I didn't know what Lee had said until long after. When Bryant's wife died, and then his son, he suffered some kind of breakdown. Ray went to see him – this was before Bryant retired, while he was just on sick leave. He told Ray about my letters and reminded him about Lee's curse. Ray had been out at the Markham house by then, he wasn't present for that part of Lee's statement, and though he had read the statement he'd not taken it as seriously as Bryant. Ray contacted me, asked me to stop bothering Bryant. He explained that he was ill and suggested I write direct to Bryant's superiors. Before I had the chance to do that, Bryant had taken out the injunction. I forwarded everything to his solicitors and asked them to act, but I left Bryant alone. I felt he'd been through enough.'

'And did Ray take your warnings seriously?'

Martyn Shaw shrugged. 'I don't know,' he said. 'Ray was up to his ears by then. Some blackmail and extortion thing. Shortly after that he went on secondment to the Met, I believe; he was away for quite a time and we lost contact. I think he was like Bryant and wanted to put this behind him. As time went on I suppose it drifted out of his mind. Until Lee died and took Bryant and three children with him.'

'I want to know about Morgan's son,' Beckett said.

'Then let me talk to Farrant. He'll just fob you off, but we know one another. He hates me just about enough to tell the truth.'

Beckett was not convinced but finally he nodded. 'Take George Mahoney with you,' he said. 'I can't spare anyone from here and he may as well earn his keep. I'll give you one try, and if you don't deliver you and Farrant will both end up charged with obstruction. I don't give a damn how I look, Shaw. None of that cuts with me.'

Martyn Shaw smiled slightly. 'I'm sure Ray Flowers likes you,' he said quietly. 'You're two of the same kind.'

Ray had been unable to settle. He knew that Beckett was due to meet Shaw and had hoped to be included, but he guessed that Beckett was finding it hard enough dealing with his superiors' disapproval as it was without calling him in to what was already a controversial meeting. George had phoned him to say that he had left Shaw there and was to pick him up later on. 'Provided our friend Beckett hasn't locked him up.'

'For what?' Ray had asked.

'Mood he was in when I left, I don't think he needs much reason.'

It was the sound that drew Ray to the window. Sharp and rasping, straight-through pipes doing little to muffle or modify the exhaust note. He looked down. The bike was parked beneath a streetlamp, the sodium lights harsh and garish on the red and chrome. The rider, black-clad and all but invisible.

Ray saw him lift his visor and look up at the window, his face pale against the black of his clothing and jaundiced by the yellow light. He gazed at Ray for a moment and then beckoned.

Pausing for just long enough to scribble a quick note to Sarah, Ray grabbed his coat, fishing in the pockets for his keys even as he ran downstairs. As he reached his car, the biker was already moving off. Ray wrenched open the door and scrambled inside, firing the engine and shifting into gear even before he'd put on his lights or fastened his seat belt. They picked up speed towards the end of the street, the biker stopping only to make certain he was still there before riding out onto the main Welford road and through the city.

Traffic was light, the rush hour long gone and the cold and intermittent rain keeping people indoors. Even

so, it was hard to keep up with the biker, who was for-
ging ahead.

Once they had passed out of the city centre and Ray
was certain they'd be heading towards Mallingham, he
called Beckett on his mobile. He still found it awkward,
even with the hands-free set, to concentrate on his driving
and deal with the phone. The scars on his hands made
fine movements awkward and at the end of the day his
fingers were always stiff. Then someone else answered.
Beckett, he was told, was in a meeting and couldn't be
disturbed.

Ray cursed angrily. He spent precious time explaining
to the officer who he was and what was going on, then
lost the signal as he hit a dead spot and had to go through
the entire procedure again.

This time, to his relief, Beckett answered him.

'We've turned off the A47 and are heading towards
Mallingham on the B459. Our ETA is about fifteen
minutes.'

'Got that, Ray. How do you want to play this one?'

'I want to get to Katie. I figure he's leading me there
but I don't know why. Don't move in, not yet. Wait until
we reach our destination.'

He felt Beckett hesitate. In Beckett's place he'd most
likely have insisted they move in now, grab the biker and
think about Katie later. He knew that Beckett was half
convinced that she was dead already.

'I'll hold back,' he told Ray, 'but once we're in
Mallingham, I'm closing down fast. I want him, Ray. We
can't afford the risk.'

It was the way Ray himself would have played it and

he felt he couldn't argue. 'Give me as much time as you can,' he said. 'You've got units all over town ready to mobilize. I'll keep the commentary going.'

He entered the outskirts of Mallingham, passing the newly built housing estates and plunging without break into the streets of back-to-back houses and Victorian factories that he had known since childhood. Twin rivers converged in Mallingham, one, the Lir, straightened and made navigable in the 1820s, now slicing the town across its centre. For a stretch the main road ran parallel to it and the biker took this route, Ray following close behind. He turned sharply beside St Augustine's Church, Ray almost overshooting the bend. Beyond this lay urban wastelands, redevelopment sites presently a battle-zone of rubble and half-demolished walls, with the odd warehouse still standing, marker points for what had once been thriving centres of trade. Ray could recall a time when the chimneys of the small town belched black smoke twenty-four seven, when the first sound you heard in the morning was the factory siren, the last thing you heard at night was the sound of the late shift making its way home and the ten-till-sixers taking their place. Some of the warehouses were being converted into flats, most too expensive for the locals to afford. Some of the factories too. Vast spaces that had housed machines and employed half the population now empty shells ready to be filled by partition walls and stainless-steel and polished-wood floors. Ray was glad that they were using these markers from his youth, but he was sad to see his home town like this, empty and silent and somehow betrayed.

Since the streets and the factories had gone it had

become more difficult to navigate, more difficult to commentate upon their route. 'Past the old bakery on Pindar Street and into Saxon Street,' he told Beckett. 'Saxon Street's now a pile of rubble with what remains of a pub on the corner. You can still see what's left of the Marston's sign.

'Next left into Martindale. St Augustine's primary school just before the junction.' He could hear Beckett talking, consulting with others and the rustle of the map. Then, 'Bugger!'

'Ray?' Beckett demanded. 'Ray, what's wrong?'

'Bollards. The end of the street's blocked off with fucking bollards. They're supposed to stop kerb-crawlers. The bike's gone straight through. I'm going to have to follow on foot.'

'Stay put. I've two units within a couple of streets of where you are.'

'And he'll be long gone. This place is a warren of one-way streets and alleyways. A bike can get through, but not a car.' He grabbed the mobile phone from its stand and hauled himself out of the car, then began to follow the bike, keeping up his commentary to Beckett and hoping that the batteries would last. Already the phone was indicating low power, the LED blinking at him every second or two. 'I don't see him and I don't hear him either, so he must have parked.'

'Watch yourself,' Beckett warned. 'Look, Ray, wait for back-up.'

'Why get me to follow if he planned to lose me? He must have clocked your people, either that or known I used the phone.'

He moved forward between the houses and out into the narrow street beyond. There were cars parked on both sides of the road and passages leading to the rear of the houses, their position shown by a deepening of the shadow. The streetlights helped little, inadequately placed and now fogged by the more rapidly falling rain.

'Any sign?' Beckett demanded.

'Nothing. No, wait a minute.' He sensed rather than saw movement in the narrow cut-through which led onto what had been another street and was now just another bombsite. Ray moved forward again, reluctant to go into the deeper blackness, even more reluctant to walk away. Behind him he could hear a car pulling up beside his own and common sense told him that he should hold on. Wait for the officers to get to him. A crunch of feet on gravel or broken glass and then footsteps running away towards the ruined buildings overrode what common sense had said and had him in hot pursuit. 'I see him,' he told Beckett, shouting hoarsely into the mobile as he cleared the alley and broke once more into the open. 'He's . . .' But he never finished what he'd been about to say. The man emerged from the shadows, detaching himself like a piece of the darkness springing into life. He turned on his heel and kicked, the booted foot catching Ray painfully on the knuckles and sending the mobile spinning into the air. Ray heard it land and shatter against broken brickwork. He almost had a chance to shout, but the hand was across his mouth and something hard pressed against the small of his back, the fragment of darkness that had attacked him solid and hard-muscled and armed.

217

Jane Adams

'Stay quiet and stay very still.' The voice was soft, seeming to insinuate itself straight into his head.

Ray then found himself being moved gently back into the shadows between the broken walls. It was in his mind that this was a bluff, that the man held nothing more lethal against his back than a length of pipe or piece of wood, but even as he thought that he knew he would not take the risk. Images of Sarah flooded into his mind and he realized that this was no time for misplaced heroics. What if this madman really had a gun? Even a knife held there just above his kidneys could be fatal. He heard footsteps thunder past only yards away and the radio crackle into life.

'Don't move and don't even breathe,' the voice whispered. 'I don't want to talk to them, only to you.'

They waited until the officer ran back the other way, his companion hurrying over to join him, their voices conveying bewilderment and, through the crackle of radio static, Ray heard Beckett's fury.

Then the man led him away, slowly, gently, one hand on his arm as though in consideration of the rough ground, the other holding whatever it was tight against his back, pressing painfully through his clothes hard against his spine.

Chapter Thirty-Eight

Farrant, leader of New Vision, lived about eighty miles from Mallingham. George drove fast on deserted roads while Martyn Shaw, stressed and jet-lagged, dozed in the seat beside him.

Farrant's house was in the middle of fenland out beyond Peterborough and towards the Wash. It sat on a small headland, the driveway crossing a bridge over a broad dyke and between flat empty fields of winter grain. The house was squat and grey, looking out over the bleak flatness of the fenland, and George guessed that on a good clear day Farrant might even be able to see the grey waters of the Wash as it flooded out into the North Sea.

George reached over and nudged his passenger back into wakefulness. Shaw murmured an apology for going to sleep, then stretched as best he could in the cramped confines of the car.

'What a bleak place.'

'In summer it can be beautiful. Vast skies and the ocean just on the horizon, but I agree that February may not be kind.'

'He's not going to want to see us.'

George shrugged. 'Does that matter? It's either us or the police. We put it to him that way, he might see sense.'

Shaw grimaced. 'I think it'll be us *and* the police,' he said. 'I can't see Beckett letting any of us off the hook.'

'Can you blame him?'

Martyn Shaw shook his head. 'No. Not in the least. I don't pretend to like this though.'

A security light came on as they got closer to the house and a dog barked from somewhere beyond the garden wall. It was just after ten p.m.

George hammered on the door. The sound echoed loudly and the barking of the dog became more frenzied. Farrant came to the door and peered through the narrow glass at its centre. It was clear that he recognized Martyn Shaw at once, for his expression changed from one of mild concern at the arrival of such late visitors to one of hatred.

'What do you want?'

'To come in would be nice,' Shaw said mildly. 'It's very cold out here, David.'

Farrant scowled at Shaw's familiarity. 'I don't want to talk to you. I've nothing to say.'

'I can wait, so can my friend here. And if we don't manage to talk to you tonight, you'll find the police camped on your doorstep tomorrow. You will anyway, but they might make less of a noise about it if you co-operate now.'

'You've no authority here. You come here threatening me? I'll call the police myself.'

Martyn Shaw shrugged his shoulders. 'Fair enough,' he said. He paused, then said, 'DI Beckett was very upset, you know, that I was the one to tell him about James. He thought you might have done him that courtesy.'

Farrant froze. 'I know nothing about him.'

'Oh, yes, you do, but I was the one who had to tell

Beckett whom he might be looking for. He wasn't pleased to think you'd been holding out on him, David. He was talking about a press conference when we left him. Scheduled for ten in the morning, I believe. You're not the only one who can manipulate the media, you know. I'd make a bet that DI Beckett's pretty good too.'

Farrant hesitated for a moment more, then unlocked the door and pulled it wide open. He stalked away from them down the hall and into the room beyond.

George raised an eyebrow at Shaw. 'You ever think of changing your profession,' he said, 'let me know.'

'I got us in,' Shaw acknowledged, 'but I think it's your turn now.'

George nodded.

'I really don't know what happened to Morgan's son,' Shaw told him. 'But I do believe he might be the one carrying on Lee's work, and I'm pretty certain Farrant suspects that too.'

Farrant was waiting for them in the living room at the back of the house. The curtains were open but the room lights blocked the view of the night beyond the window, merely reflecting their own images back on them. Farrant clutched a cut-glass tumbler and the ice in it rattled as his hands shook. He offered them nothing, did not even invite them to sit down. George did so anyway, taking up position in a winged armchair while Shaw perched on the arm of a sofa on the opposite side of the room.

'What happened to Morgan's son?' George asked him.

'How the hell should I know?'

221

'You worshipped Morgan, denied the new Prophet when he took over. You can't tell me you didn't keep in touch with his son.'

'Where did James go to?' Shaw asked him. 'I know he went into rehab. I know Morgan had him drugged up to the eyeballs, pumped him full of God knows what, until the poor kid nearly lost his mind.'

'That wasn't Morgan. He didn't give James drugs. That was Harry Lee.'

'But Morgan colluded,' Martyn Shaw persisted. 'Morgan himself told me. "Anything it takes," he said. He had no scruples, David, not even where his own son was involved.'

'You know nothing about it. You weren't even there.'

'No, but you were,' George put in. 'You know what went on. Perhaps you even colluded with Morgan and Lee. Perhaps that's why you weren't at the Markham house that night. Did Morgan warn you? Did you know those people were going to die?'

'I believe you did, David.' Shaw picked up on George's words. 'I'm certain that you were warned. That you could have prevented it all.'

'Twelve people died,' George added quietly. 'Why weren't you among them, Farrant? In fact, where were you that night?'

Farrant looked outraged. He slammed his glass down on a nearby table and strode across to the door, pulling it open. 'Get out of my house,' he yelled. 'Get the hell out of my house or I'll call the police. Now!'

George glanced across the room at Martyn Shaw and then slowly shook his head. 'It's been a long drive tonight,' he said, 'and it's going to be a long drive back. My friend over there is jet-lagged and rather upset to hear what you've been saying about him to the media. I don't think we're ready to go. Not until you tell us what you know.'

He got up and went over to Farrant's sideboard, sorting thoughtfully through the bottles. 'Drink, Martyn?'

'Wouldn't mind.'

Shaw slipped off the arm of the sofa and settled himself along the length of it, stretching out and crossing his booted feet at the ankles. 'What's he got then, George?'

'Half-decent malt . . . Oh, I was wrong, a very decent malt. You like Macallan's, Martyn?'

Farrant strode back across the room and snatched the bottle from George's hand.

'James Morgan is not violent,' he declared furiously. 'He left the Markham house because he had a breakdown. He's not a murderer. You want your killer, then you and I both know who he is. That child Lee brought to the house. His so-called angel. Lee was a perverted monster, destroying and dirtying everything he ever touched. It wasn't Morgan and it wasn't Morgan's son.'

'And where is James Morgan?' George demanded.

'How the hell should I know? Morgan checked him into a place called Friar's Retreat. Some privately owned thing down in Kent. After Morgan died . . . after Morgan was supposed to have died and the bills weren't being paid any more, they moved him to Briargate and then I think on to somewhere else. I heard tell he ended up back at Carlton Hayes before they shut that down. I don't know after that. The last time I saw James Morgan was almost seven years ago. He didn't remember who I was. He didn't remember who his father was. He could tell you nothing about Harry Lee.'

'Did you ask him?'

Farrant shrugged. 'Yes, I asked him. I asked him what Lee was really trying to do. He swore he didn't know. I don't think he even knew what I was talking about. After that, I thought it best to leave him alone.'

'And what else?' Shaw persisted. 'Did you ask him about the money, David?'

Farrant stiffened. 'I don't know what you mean. What money?'

'The money Morgan took from his followers. The money he invested in offshore accounts. The money that you believed was rightly yours because you were certain that Morgan would name you as his heir after I had gone.'

'And so I would have been. Morgan changed his will after you betrayed him. I saw the will. I saw Lee counter-sign it. Morgan pledged control of the Eyes of God to me.'

'And the money that went with that no doubt. Morgan made some wise investments as I remember.'

Farrant's jaw set tightly. 'I know nothing about that,' he declared. 'Anyway, why are you asking me? You destroyed that final will. You took over what was rightly mine. You hold everything that Morgan had bequeathed to me. You want answers to that, Martyn Shaw, then look to yourself for them.'

Shaw got up and paced across to the window. He stood close to Farrant, examining the man thoughtfully as if he were some new kind of insect. 'That's just it, Farrant. I don't have what Morgan left. And I knew long ago that he'd just faked his death and would want to collect. Maybe he did, I don't know, but when I took control, if that's what you can call it, I had nothing. Morgan owned a little place in Wales. It was his private property. He had it as a holiday place and I eventually got them to release the deeds of that, though it took for ever to go through probate because of the ongoing investigation. Meantime I'd held down two jobs and had an overdraft the size of the national debt just finishing university. I sold the house and used the money to pay off my debts and get us started again. We lived in a terraced place in Nottingham for another two years, gradually repairing the damage Morgan had done to what was left of his followers. But one thing he had taught me was how to play the markets and as soon as we could scrape the cash together that's what I did.' He grinned. 'I proved to have quite a talent for predicting futures. But what Lee and Morgan hid stayed hidden. In that, I'm as wise as you.'

He sighed as though his journey and the trials of the day had suddenly caught up with him. 'Write it down,' he said. 'The last place you know that James Morgan was resident. All the rehab centres and hospitals before that. The names of anyone who might have treated him.'

He glanced across at George. 'Anything else?' he asked.

'Probably, but we'll let Beckett ask the rest. That will do for now.'

They watched as Farrant, his hands still shaking, wrote out the list they wanted. It covered two A4 sheets by the time he had done, as if the act of writing, once begun, was difficult to stop.

'I know nothing more,' he declared when he had finished. 'Now go. Just go and leave me in peace.'

'You didn't ask,' Shaw commented, 'but I expect the other will was destroyed in the explosion. Funny really.'

Farrant said nothing. He stood at the door until they had returned to their car and then slammed it hard.

'These investments,' George asked. 'You think that's why Dignan is interested?'

'Your boss? We've met, you know,' Shaw said. Then: 'I would guess so, yes. Like Farrant, everyone assumed that they had transferred to me. You obviously know that we were investigated?'

George nodded.

'Well, we came up clean. I had nothing to hide and I don't now. I never had a penny from Morgan except the money he gave me for rent in my first year at uni. And that I'd always intended to pay back. The proceeds from his house helped to build the Eyes of God as it is now. My books are clean.'

'And what was Morgan dealing in?'

'I don't know for certain. There were rumours and there were people who approached me once they thought I'd taken over. I believe he was dealing arms. I don't want to think that. He was my mentor, my family, for a long time.'

'You say that and yet you seem barely to have known James Morgan.'

'James lived with his mother. He came to live with Morgan only after she died. Her death almost sent him over the edge then. He wasn't the most stable of people. Sensitive, scared of living. He idolized his father. Morgan used to see him regularly and take him out, buy him stuff, spoil him rotten. He loved his mother. I guess she was the stable element in his life, but his father made out like he was the provider of fun, of all the stuff he wanted. It must have made it difficult.'

George nodded. It was a game he'd seen many divorced couples play to a greater or lesser extent. 'And the will?' he asked. 'The one that was destroyed in the Markham house?'

Martyn smiled gently and reached into his coat. 'Here,' he said. 'Lee's angel had it. When Morgan deserted him, he gave it to me.'

Sarah and Mitch arrived to collect Ray only to find the office lights left on and the place deserted. A scribbled note on the desk said, 'Following a lead. Call later, Beckett knows.' They were puzzling over where he might be when the phone began to ring. Sarah reached over and switched on the speakerphone. It was Rowena.

'Oh, hello,' she said. 'Is Ray there? He said he might be working late.'

'Good question,' Sarah told her. 'Anything I can do?'

'It's Martha really. She's been talking to her people. The ones who come to the shelter. Ray mentioned a motorbike and this old guy remembered it and the rider. He's apparently good for a touch every now and then.'

'He has a description?' Sarah asked her.

'Yes, mid-twenties or a little younger. Shoulder-length dark hair and brown eyes. He's slim and about medium height, but the important thing is his tattoos. Apparently, Fred, that's the old guy, he met him coming out of a tattooist one day. She doesn't have a shop front, only does clients recommended or who hear about her by word of mouth. Fred knows her because she'll give him a cup of tea if he turns up at the right time. Anyway, he recognized the biker and asked Tina, that's the tattooist, about his tattoos. She wouldn't tell him at first but finally she let on that they were faces. Portraits.'

'You can do that with tattoos?'

'Apparently. There's some special shading technique. Anyway, this Tina says that his back is covered with them. They're the portraits of children and the pictures she copied were from newspaper clippings.'

'The children Lee killed?' Sarah guessed.

'I don't know,' Rowena admitted. 'But Martha thought you ought to be told.'

Sarah thanked her and when she was off the phone dialled Beckett's number. Mitch had gone pale.

'What is it?' Sarah asked her.

'The portraits on his back,' Mitch said. 'In Irene's dream. The angel had the images of children carved into his skin.'

Sarah regarded her thoughtfully. 'That's not as much as I'd like to do to him,' she said. 'Hello. Beckett, this is

Sarah Gordon. We haven't met but I'm sure you've heard of me.'

She told him quickly what Rowena had related to her and then asked him, 'Where's Ray? He left me a note to say he was following some lead and that you knew about it.'

Beckett hesitated long enough for Sarah to reach her own conclusions. 'You don't know where he is, do you? He's off somewhere on his own.'

'We did know,' Beckett assured her. 'He followed the biker back to Mallingham. We had him under observation and then we lost him.'

'I'm coming over,' Sarah told him. 'And you can tell me just how the entire police force in Mallingham could manage to lose someone the size of Ray Flowers.'

She slammed the phone down before he could protest, then searched her pocket for her car keys. 'Bloody incompetent . . .' She stopped, her voice breaking suddenly. 'I think you'd better drive,' she said to Mitch. 'I don't think I could see too well just now.'

George had called Dignan and Shaw had used a pen-light torch to read out the list that Farrant had given them. Dignan had promised to get on to it right away and keep them informed.

'Isn't it a bit late tonight?' Shaw commented when they had finished.

George laughed. 'Dignan doesn't sleep,' he said. 'He rests for a few hours a day in a coffin filled with his native soil and he's never thought that other people might need a little more.'

Shaw laughed. 'Well, this other person does. I've lost track of the last time I did more than doze.'

'We'd better get in touch with Beckett,' George told him. 'Keep him up to date. The number's in the directory.'

Beckett was clearly as exhausted as Martyn Shaw, but his news put all thought of sleep from their mind.

'We lost him,' Beckett repeated when he'd finished telling them what happened. 'We were literally one, two minutes behind. We found what was left of his mobile phone, it had been smashed into a wall, but there was no sign of Ray. Sarah Gordon's on her way here. I tried to put her off but she was in no mood to listen.'

'Ray will be all right,' George told him with more confidence than he felt. 'He was in the force for a long time.'

'So was Bryant,' Beckett reminded him.

Chapter Thirty-Nine

Ray Flowers was not amused and, had he been forced to admit it, he was afraid, though the two emotions competed so equally that he could not have said which one had control. The young man had guided him away from the building site and through another empty lot, moving from shadow to shadow with the certainty of a cat stalking prey. Behind him, Ray could hear increasing activity as the first two officers were joined by others. A police car, siren wailing now, as brash as the first one had been stealthy, careened into the narrow street and screeched to a halt just before it hit the bollards.

'You must be popular,' his companion commented.

Ray snorted. 'I'm an ex-police officer. Loyalty means something.'

'Even one who betrayed his superiors?'

'They were corrupt. They deserved it.'

The younger man seemed to be considering that, because he fell silent again, just urged Ray forward with the pressure of the unseen weapon in the middle of his back.

Again Ray pondered heroics. Again he dismissed the idea. He wasn't lithe or fit enough for that sort of thing and he had felt the wire-sprung muscles of the younger man's arms, seen the speed with which he could move. Ray knew himself to be outmatched.

'In here.'

'Here' was an old garage with broken doors and peeling paint. The young man pushed Ray inside and reached to close the door with his free hand, then abruptly he moved away, releasing Ray from the threat of the thing pressed into his back.

Ray turned. Anger overriding fear. 'What the fuck do you think you're playing at?'

'I needed to get you here. I didn't want to be followed and you had me followed.'

'Damn right I did. What the hell else should I have done?'

The young man's eyes flickered away from him and then his gaze came back to rest upon Ray's face. Even in the dark he was aware of its intensity.

'You could have trusted me,' he said to Ray, his voice soft and rather sad.

'And why should I do that?'

He felt the young man shrug. Even though his eyes were getting used to the darkness, the black-clad figure blended into the surrounding gloom so well that he could barely discern his outline.

The young man moved, bent to lift something from the floor. The door opened, revealing a ramp leading down, and he gestured for Ray to precede him, pausing to relock the doors behind them before moving down the ramp to yet another set of doors.

Inside, Ray let his gaze travel over the paintings on the walls. The sheer size of this crypt, hidden beneath the streets, astounded him. And there was Katie, sitting on what looked like a raised dais, an altar almost, at one end of the room, beneath the image of a massive winged figure, hands outstretched as if in greeting.

'Ray!'

Katie sounded delighted. She ran to him and threw her arms around his neck. 'I didn't think he'd really fetch you. He said he would but I didn't believe him.'

Still irritated by the entire affair, Ray detached her and held her by the hands. 'Do you know how many people are out looking for you?' he demanded. 'Do you know how your parents feel right now? I took a copy of your note to them and your mother just couldn't stop crying. Your dad looks ten years older.' He turned from her to face the man who stood quietly as though waiting his turn. 'Just what the hell is going on?'

For the next hour Ray listened as they talked to him about the dead boys and the 'other one' that Nathan felt was so close by. He had heard nothing about Morgan's son and so all of this was new to him. He listened, feeling the patterns falling into place and a new set of questions forming in his mind.

'Nathan,' he said. 'Nathan was the name of Lee's final victim.'

'It's a name. I use it.'

'And what *is* your name? Your given name?'

Nathan shook his head slowly as though he didn't know.

Ray sighed, very tired and deeply frustrated. 'You said you're keeping her here for her safety,' he said, gesturing towards Katie. 'And yet you know that you

233

can't. I will allow that your motives were good enough, but your methods are all wrong. Why not come to us, tell us what you know and ask for help?'

He shook his head. 'You would have locked me away,' he said.

'Who told you that? Who fed your mind with so much crap?' Receiving no answer, Ray carried on, speaking slowly and carefully, knowing how important it was that his words got through. 'There's a child out there, dead or waiting to die, and a young woman here who doesn't know what's going to happen to her or if you can stop it. I think you've seen enough death. I don't believe you want any of this to happen.'

'I can't save him. It will be too late.'

'Where did Lee kill the boys?'

'At the Markham house. Down in the cellar. It collapsed after the explosion.'

'The Markham house!' Ray was genuinely shocked. 'The ones who lived there, did they know?'

Nathan shook his head. 'Some of them, I think. Others did not want to know. Lee never wanted me talking to them. I lived there, but he kept me separate. Me and James.'

'The cellar. You're sure it can't be accessed now?'

'Certain. I went there after I heard that Harry Lee had died. I knew . . . I was afraid it might all start again. That Morgan would come back. I thought that Harry might have sent his soul to him, but it wasn't Morgan. It was Morgan's son.'

Nathan stopped abruptly, and for a while no one

spoke. Then Katie looked long and hard at him and said, 'Tell him everything, Nathan. Tell him the rest.'

'I wasn't the only one. I mean the only one they thought might be the avatar. Lee . . . He was my father, at least that's what he said. Lee wanted it to be me, but for a long time Morgan argued that it was James, and then something happened. I think they might have tried the ritual or done something and it went wrong, and they changed their minds about the other one. About James Morgan.'

'Tell me about him. What do you know about him now?'

'He's older than me. Taller than me. Stronger. And he moves like smoke and sometimes, sometimes I can hear his thoughts. He saw what I saw back then, he sees what I see now, like we're the same mind, and I know that Lee did not send his soul to Morgan. He called out to Morgan's son and I believe he found him.'

Ray frowned. He wasn't happy with all of this talk of possession, though he had to admit that there had been times in his life when he had seen and experienced things he could not easily explain. And, as he'd told Beckett, often it didn't seem to matter what you believed, you were just an observer, not an actor.

'You have to come with me,' he said to Nathan at last. 'You have to release me and let me take Katie to Beckett. Come with us, tell him what you've told me. He's been talking to Martyn Shaw and I think if the two of you meet we might be able to get somewhere. Save more lives.'

Nathan gazed down at the floor as if the answer was to be found there. Then he nodded slowly. 'All right,' he said. 'I'll come. In a little while.'

It was after two a.m. by the time Dignan called back. The incident room was as crowded as if it were eight o'clock in the morning just before the early briefing.

Beckett had left most of his team to get a night's sleep. There was nothing they could usefully be doing that wasn't being done by uniform and tomorrow would be a busy day, sifting through the information that the past few hours had generated. Interviewing Farrant and his people.

George and Martyn Shaw had arrived back just after one. Beckett wondered what speed George must have been doing to achieve that but thought it better not to ask. Dignan had worked wonders in the brief time, but then, Beckett thought, he probably had the resources and didn't seem to have anyone telling him what he couldn't do.

'James Morgan was committed as a voluntary patient at the age of seventeen,' Dignan told them. 'His father told the doctors that James had a drug problem but that he knew nothing more. The doctor who had care of James, a Dr Carpenter, wrote in his notes that he believed the father knew more than he was letting on but commented that it was not unusual for parents to be in denial. James was psychotic and delusional. He told doctors that he believed himself to be some kind of messiah who was going to save the world. His tox results revealed cocaine, amphetamine and possibly heroin, though as you know that metabolizes in something like forty-eight hours, so the results were inconclusive.

'There was an initial diagnosis of latent schizophrenia. He heard voices, was deeply paranoid, but the tox results cast doubt on that. His symptoms were as consistent with a mind screwed up by chemicals as they were with schizophrenia.'

'Was the schizophrenia diagnosis ever confirmed?' George asked.

'No. In fact later in James's mental health career no fewer than three doctors cast doubt upon the analysis. James was destroyed by the drugs his father and Lee administered and by their . . . well, brainwashing is probably as good a term as any. They took an already vulnerable young man and systematically took him apart.'

'And what happened to him, after Friar's Retreat?'

'Half a dozen other hospitals. He was finally admitted back to Briargate and treated in their drug-dependency unit. He'd been through treatment before but always on release got back on the stuff. This time though, something seemed to stick. He came off and stayed off. Eventually he went back to live in the community and they even found him a job. His delusions hadn't completely left him, he was still excessively religious, but he seemed peaceful. Content, even. Until about six weeks ago.'

'And what happened then?'

'One day, the 18th as it happens, a month before Lee's death, James didn't show up at work and no one's seen him since.'

'What turned things around for him?' Beckett asked.

'He learned to paint. It seemed to be the answer for him. He didn't have much talent by all accounts, but as therapy it did have its merits. Before that he made collages. He used the wings of moths. He'd lure them into his room by leaving his curtains open and having the light switched on, then he'd pull off their wings when they came crashing down. He called them his angels.'

They were all silent for a time when Dignan had signed off, then Shaw spoke softly. 'Not delusional. Indoctrinated. Brainwashed and drugged. Then when he broke down they shifted their attention to the other one, the boy Lee called his angel.' He grimaced. 'I hear voices, see visions and they call me a prophet. James Morgan—'

'You still function in the real world,' George interrupted harshly. 'You have control over what you do. Question it. And you don't demand the death of children to satisfy your need for power.'

'So James Morgan becomes prime suspect,' Beckett said slowly. 'You think he has Katie and Ray?'

'I don't know about Ray,' Shaw told him, 'but Katie, no. I think she's with the angel.'

'Angel!' Beckett couldn't help but be contemptuous. 'OK, so there are two of them out there, maybe equally dangerous.' He turned angrily to Shaw. 'What kind of an organization is this? How do you live with yourself?'

'*Was* this?' Shaw retorted. He sighed. 'When I took over what was left. . . . All that was left really was a group of frightened people looking for direction. Those who had somewhere else to go mostly did and tried to forget they'd ever been a part of all this. The ones who were left were shell-shocked. They'd given their lives to Morgan. Their money too. Many had cut themselves off from family and had nothing to go back to.

'Farrant is right about one thing. I did throw away Morgan and Lee's teachings. I did wipe the slate clean and turn the Eyes of God into something unrecognizable to the likes of him. And I have not one single regret about that.' He turned to Mitch. 'I am so sorry about Irene and Bryn. I truly thought they'd be able to put the past behind them.'

'I don't know,' Mitch said sadly. 'I don't believe they wanted Morgan back in the end. And I know they didn't want what's happening now. I think they killed themselves because they couldn't deal with the guilt. If they'd talked about what they knew earlier, the children might not have died . . .'

At that point the phone began to ring and it brought the first good news they'd heard in a long time. Ray was on the line and he had Katie with him.

Chapter Forty

Ray looked exhausted when he and Katie walked into the incident room, but all eyes were on Katie. It was Beckett who spoke first.

'Are you OK?'

Katie nodded briefly, then strode across the room to where Martyn Shaw was standing. She was clearly furious about something. Her blue eyes flashed coldly and even Shaw had the grace to look perturbed.

Anger had lent her more fluency than usual, though she still stumbled over the words. 'Nathan said you helped him but I don't think you did. I think you just gave him money and hoped he'd go away. You turned Nathan into just another down-and-out. He might have had money, but that was all he had. No one to care about him, no family, nothing. It wasn't his fault, what happened, but you just thought out of sight, out of mind, instead of dealing with him like he mattered.'

Everyone fell silent, shocked by her outburst, but Shaw just nodded.

'You're right,' he said. 'I didn't know what I could do with Nathan. That way I'm guilty as the rest.'

'Nathan?' Beckett questioned.

'The kid on the bike,' Ray told him.

'Harry Lee's angel,' Shaw said.

Ray finally broke the silence that followed this

announcement. 'I thought I'd persuaded him to come with us, but when we left the basement he disappeared. Slipped off into the darkness and that was it. We heard the bike roar away.'

'He's gone looking for the other one,' Katie said.

'Katie says he confessed to killing Morgan. He thought that if he did that it would make it all stop. He's spent night after night trying to second-guess Morgan and his son. I wanted to bring him here. I thought if I could persuade him to come back with us we might get somewhere.'

'What we all need now,' George said, 'is sleep, and we need to get Katie back to her parents. I take it you've been in touch with them?'

'Of course. Katie talked to them. But, George, I don't want them left at the hotel. We need a safe house,' Ray said.

George nodded. 'Looks as though you'll have someone sharing your accommodation,' he said to Shaw. 'I think that might be best.'

'I've told the Fellowses to expect you. Forgive me, George, but I don't think I can handle much more just now.' He looked across at Beckett. 'Any objections to this?'

'Got enough on my hands. And I think you're right about the hotel and,' he said, turning to George, 'about needing sleep. We'll speak in the morning. George, I'm going to need a statement from Katie and from you and Martyn. Make arrangements, will you? You've got Emma Thorn's number. I think she can deal with it.'

George nodded.

Ray was gazing out of the window into the deserted street, wondering where Nathan was. He was angry with himself for being fooled again.

Chapter Forty-One

Mid-afternoon and the rain had been falling steadily for over an hour. Nathan could feel the other one. He was close by, the feel of him as strong as any scent, feral and pungent in Nathan's consciousness.

The police had found his home, as Nathan knew they would once he let Ray and Katie leave. Ray would have to tell and Nathan accepted that. He was used to travelling light and all the things in life that really mattered to him could be loaded onto his bike or stuffed into a backpack. He was above Mallingham now, sheltering beneath a galvanized water tank on the flat roof of a disused factory. From the rooftop he could see over the west side of the town, right across to where the twin rivers joined and carved through its heart, the long straight gash of captured water diminished to nothing from this high up.

Nathan wore a long coat over his leathers, khaki green and caped, the kind an Australian stockman might favour. Its waxed surface protected his black jacket and broke his outline, grey-green against washed-out metal, moss-encrusted concrete and leaden, unforgiving sky.

He knew that James would come back, as he had done so many times already, to where Nathan had been living. James had moved across Mallingham, settling for a night here, two nights there, a nomadic existence forced upon him by circumstance and, Nathan guessed, by Morgan. By contrast, Nathan had lived in his cellar beneath the building site for almost a year. Finding it when the demolition stopped and left the lower floor of a pub and the crypt intact.

His stillness against the restless modification going on around him had made him so much easier to find. James had sensed him, been drawn to him by the same emotional scent that brought Nathan to this place now, overlooking the streets leading to his former home. And he knew he had one advantage over James. He, Nathan, could move across the city at any height, above the ground, upon it or below. Travelling by routes that James would never venture to use. Morgan and Lee had left him with a fear of many things – high places, confinement underground, loud noises and bright light. If he could once fix on James, see him rather than just sense his presence moving like smoke blown in the wind, then Nathan knew that he could follow. James would know he was there, but he would not know how to lose him. Since Lee and Morgan had corrupted his mind, James had never raised his eyes to look up or been able to face the monsters that bred, in his mind at least, below the solid ground.

For an hour, Nathan barely moved, occasionally shifting his position against the wall behind the tank. His gaze scanning restlessly, from one street to the next. From one movement to another. He saw the police searching the wasteground where he had smashed Ray's mobile phone. Saw them moving in and out through the garage that led down into his cellar. Saw people open their doors to examine the activity, being forced back inside by the driving rain, and he felt James edging closer to him, street by street, shadow by shadow, as the afternoon wore on and the rain slanted in the strengthening wind. He shifted his weight slightly, turned up the collar of his coat against the cold and then settled back to wait some more.

Beckett had found Tina. Nathan's skin artist was not what he had expected. She was small and slight with long dark hair and a pretty oval face. Celtic black-work decorated her upper arms and a tiny, elaborate knot had been worked just above her cheekbone close to her left eye, like an beauty spot whose intricacies could be seen only if you moved in close.

The walls of her workroom were decorated with photographs of her designs. More were concealed in black portfolios stacked on every available surface and despite the fact that it was an ordinary room in a terraced house, the work area itself was spotless. An autoclave took pride of place on a shelf. Sterile packs of new needles lay in a blue bowl alongside tiny pots ready for the pigment. She had a framed certificate on the wall stating that she was registered with the local council and another from the board of health and safety.

And she was good. Even to the uninitiated, such as Beckett, who generally placed tattoos in the same category as seaside rock and kiss-me-quick hats.

'I'm an artist,' Tina had said, and, looking at her work, Beckett had to admit this was true.

'Do you ever work with paint?' he asked her. 'On canvas or anything like that?'

Tina smiled nervously. 'Yeah, some. I do bike tanks too. Always wanted to do his but he wouldn't have it. Said it was right the way it was.'

'What bike is it?' Ray asked her. 'I know it's a café racer, 1950s styling, but that's all I managed to see.'

'It's a Norton. Dominator, the 650 sports model, he said. I know it was loud. Fast too and it was really old – 1960 something.'

'Really old,' Becket muttered under his breath. He made a note about the bike, its make and model.

'You keep pictures of all your work?' Ray asked.

She shifted uncomfortably. 'Most,' she said. 'But not his, he wouldn't let me. It was some of the best work I ever did, but it was weird, you know? A lot of my stuff I submit to trade mags. It's good publicity if they show your shots, but I'd never have sent those in. Too strange.'

'And it never seemed more than just "strange". That someone should have the faces of dead children inked on his body?'

She shrugged. 'Look, you've got to understand, I was nine years old when those kids died and I wasn't even living round here. All I knew, they could be his brothers. I didn't ask, he didn't say. He just turned up one night about two years ago and said he'd heard that I was good and could I work from photographs. The last two were newspaper clippings. I didn't finish the second one. I'd realized who the kids were by then and I'd got scared.'

'Photographs?' Ray questioned. 'Actual photographs or newspaper clippings?'

'No, the real thing. Glossy five by fours. They were pictures of the boys and other people. He had a selection and I chose the ones I could work from. Most were like, you know, candid shots. Kids playing when they weren't taking any notice of the camera. Nice and natural. Who-ever took them knew what he was doing.'

'It didn't occur to you to call the police?' Beckett said heavily.

She nodded. 'I did call, twice. I gave a description of him, but I didn't give my name. I said I thought he might be the killer but I couldn't tell them anything like where he lived or even what he was called. Just that he was some guy with dark hair and brown eyes and skin art all down his back.'

Beckett sighed and exchanged a glance with Ray. They both knew that such a call would find its way to the bottom of the pile when it came to follow-ups. Such a vague description, with no personal details, would be inputted onto the computer system, but unless there was a cross-match it would sit there while more promising leads were pursued.

'Did you tackle him about this? What did you say to him?'

'I asked him straight out. No. No, I didn't. He said something like, "You think it's me, don't you?" What could I say? Look, he scared me. I thought of moving away, then I thought, well, where would I go? I just kept the door locked and my personal alarm where I could reach it.'

'And do you think that now? That he's the killer?'

She looked at Ray, an odd expression on her face, as though she was trying hard to work it all out and getting nowhere. Finally, she shook her head. 'It doesn't feel right,' she said. 'He was always so gentle. Quiet. I mean,

I know that doesn't mean anything. People said Ted Bundy was a nice guy, but, I don't know.' She shrugged. 'I liked him. I liked him a whole lot. Sometimes, you know, I think he came close to asking me out.'

'But not to telling you his name?'

She smiled, catching the mockery in Beckett's voice. 'Yeah. He called himself Angel. You know, like on the vampire show on TV. I figured he must be a fan or it was some joke about him riding an old bike. Or maybe he'd had hippie-type parents, you know. I was at school with a girl called Peace Windsong. She had a sister called Bliss something or other.' She hesitated, then said, 'I don't want it to be him.'

The safe house was about nine miles from Mallingham, set well back from the country road with a high wall surrounding it on three sides and a thorn hedge on the other. It was not the kind of place you'd come upon by accident and the sign on the gate described it as a management training centre, a use it was put to from time to time, though no one going on courses there would be returning to banks or corporations to put their new-found skills to the test.

There was a fair amount of tension between Katie's parents and Martyn Shaw, but the house was large enough for them to stay apart if they wanted. After lunch, however, common sense had begun to take over and an uneasy truce been drawn up between them, fed mainly by Katie's curiosity. The thought that Martyn Shaw might know something about her background, her natural parents, even her original name, was something Katie could not pass up and her parents knew that it would be unfair not to allow them to talk.

'I didn't know you,' Shaw told her. 'I'm sorry, but I can tell you very little. Bryn mentioned a woman with a young child. She'd come to a couple of open meetings and then visited the Markham house from time to time. Bryn and Irene left Markham about three months before the explosion, though. Irene's mother was terminally ill. They stayed with relatives who lived close by so that Irene could help take care of her. I don't think Lee was sorry to see them go. They were always loyal to Morgan, and I don't think they liked Harry much or his influence.'

'And this woman,' Lisa Fellows asked, 'did they know her name?'

'Julie or Julia, I believe, but they didn't recall a last name. Morgan was never keen on last names, he said it was patriarchal and confining. Names were borrowed things, we gave them to our children, but they should be free to cast them aside as they grew and be able to choose for themselves. It wasn't unusual for people who joined the organization to pick a new name and often people joining after that would only ever know them by that name. Records weren't kept. It was a mess, really.'

'And did you know my name?' Katie asked him hopefully.

Martyn shook his head. 'I'm sorry, sweetheart. If Irene and Bryn were still around I'd suggest you talk to them. But a lot of people came to meetings. Those who went further and joined the Eyes often went to great lengths to leave their past and their families behind.'

'Seems to be a common trait of religious cults,' Guy Fellows said angrily. 'Brainwashing, separation.'

'Of some, yes,' Shaw agreed. 'I have a rule that all members of my organization contact their families at least once a week. Even if it's just a quick phone call, I want them to maintain links with the outside. I actively encourage it. We have trust funds set up to put our kids through university without them getting into debt. They're not tied to us. They're free to do their own thing and leave when they want, come back again if they want. The Eyes of God has open doors, Guy. I won't have the same ethos as Harry Lee. I don't think I could live with that.'

'Sounds very idealistic,' Guy said, the sarcasm in his voice unmistakable.

Martyn took his comments at face value. 'Oh, it is,' he said. 'Though I don't expect you to believe that. Why should you?'

'Why the Eyes of God?' Katie wanted to know.

Martyn smiled at her. 'Because we believe that we're gathering information for the divine,' he said. 'That God is not some omniscient being, but a working, changing, ever-evolving power and as part of that power we should keep our eyes wide open to all possibilities. Our eyes, our ears, our minds, our souls, however you want to put it. And because the eye has been a symbol of divine protection for as long as mankind has used symbols. Morgan believed that in the beginning. There was none of this talk of super beings or messiahs or avatars. Morgan taught that we were all equal because we all had a spark of the angelic within us.' He sighed deeply. 'If he had kept that belief, then none of this would have happened.

No one would have died. I don't know if I can ever make that right.'

'Why should you feel guilty about it?' Lisa wanted to know.

'If I'd realized sooner what Harry Lee was doing, I might have been able to warn someone. If they'd have listened.'

He had been trying to listen to their voices, Harry and his father, trying to hear what they wanted him to do, but they sounded so far away. When he crept in at the window and took the boy out, they were so clear. He had decorated the room, left the paintings they told him to leave. He brought the boy here but now the messages were confused, Lee's presence not so dominant as it had previously been, the voices in his head muted and unclear. And it was so cold in the warehouse where he had taken shelter. James wanted to go home.

He had tied the boy up and left him in the corner in the back room. Covered him with a blanket to keep him warm. And waited. And when he went in to see the boy, the child cried and moaned at him and stared, pleading into his face, and James had covered his eyes and gagged his mouth so that he did not have to see or hear. He waited patiently for the voice within that spoke from Lee's soul to tell him what to do and how everything should be.

He had left the light on last night, waiting for the moths to fly in through the window. But none came. It rained and it was cold and dark. Maybe, he thought, they

*don't fly when it's too cold. Maybe his angels were frozen
and would never fly again, but by morning the words
were clear. The other one had to die before he could
move on. The other one had the girl. As dawn broke he
went out to look for Nathan.*

Nathan could feel him now, he was on the move again
and shifting fast through the streets towards the place
where Nathan had lived. Nathan moved too, sliding back
through the broken skylight and dropping back onto the
stairs. He ran down, careful to avoid the rotting wood and
the pools of water on the concrete floor where the rain
had been driven through the ruined windows. He slipped
the coat from his shoulders and hid it under the tarpaulin
that concealed his bike, then ran from the building keeping to the deepening shadow close to the walls.

There was a brief stretch of open land, broken by
winter scrub and half-demolished walls. Just four o'clock,
but the rain had brought an early twilight and Nathan
moved easily, invisible and swift.

He climbed back up onto a factory wall, running
along the length of it, balancing with the confidence of a
gymnast on the blue bricks of its curving surface, then
down again and into the road where Ray had parked his
car the night before.

He could see the police, no longer searching now. A
couple of them shared a flask, drinking tea in the lee of a
house wall. Two others stood beside the garage doors,
but the rest had gone. Nathan had watched them go, the
searchers withdrawn for the night now that the always

uncertain daylight had all but disappeared. Just these four, then, enough though to frighten James and maybe flush him into the open.

Nathan felt the other one move out from between the houses. He moved as Nathan did, swiftly, in short bursts of speed, always finding the next cover before he left the first. And then Nathan felt him halt suddenly and, leaning out from behind the wall, glimpsed him, standing no more than twenty yards away, his body half concealed in shadow. Shock had made him careless though. He had seen the police standing beside the garage doors and realized that Nathan's hiding place was no longer secret. Nathan could feel the panic rising inside him, and the questions. He had known where to find Nathan, known just where Katie was going to be, and now that certainty had gone.

One last glance at the four officers, fixing their position in his mind, and Nathan stepped out from shelter.

James whirled to face him, his face a picture of bewilderment. For a moment Nathan felt pity for him, then he remembered the children and the moment was gone.

'She's not there,' he told James quietly. 'They took her far away from here. Somewhere you'll never get to her.'

James Morgan moved then, he turned and ran, and Nathan followed, taking to the roof tops once again, following where his angel brother led.

Chapter Forty-Two

Katie was restless. It was fully dark now and the household had settled in for the night. George had joined them for dinner and he and her father were now comfortably ensconced with a bottle of whisky, swapping army yarns. She had all but forgotten that her father had been in the forces and it was strange to hear him talking about it now. Her mother was flipping through a stack of magazines that George had brought in for her. It was rare for Lisa to bother with magazines, she never bought them at home, but had been genuinely pleased when George turned up with them. It was yet another sign, Katie thought, of the dislocation which the family had undergone. She had been studying *Hamlet* at school this year and there was a phrase in it, something about the times being out of joint. Katie hadn't really understood what it meant until now.

She pulled the heavy curtain aside and peered out of the massive window. A man with a large dog glanced across at her and then walked on. It was another odd thought, that she now had armed guards patrolling the house and grounds keeping her safe.

So why did she feel so bad?

Martyn Shaw was across the room staring at the television set, though Katie could tell that he was paying little attention to the programme. She flopped down beside him on the sofa.

'He'll still want me. He'll know I'm not with Nathan.'

Shaw turned his head to look at her. He nodded. 'I think that's likely.'

'He won't find you here,' George assured her.

'That's what I mean. I should be in Mallingham.'

'He needs the boys first.'

Katie shook her head. 'Last time. Three boys and then me. Not all six first.'

George leaned forward, suddenly attentive. 'You have a point,' he said. 'I hadn't thought of it that way.'

Katie's mother stood up suddenly, the magazines falling to the floor. She was well ahead of George. 'Oh no,' she said. 'I know just what you're thinking. You're talking about using her as bait. No way. There's no way you're doing that.'

George shook his head slowly but his gaze never left Katie's face. 'Katie's right though,' he said. 'Though I'd not thought of using her. Only of making James and Nathan think that we were. We can find a WPC in Mallingham who matches her for height and colouring. Bring Katie to Mallingham, substitute the other and then bring Katie back here.'

Lisa stared at him as if he had gone mad, but Katie nodded. 'We've got to do it,' she said. 'I'm not scared . . . Not really.'

'How can you guarantee that the killer will take the bait anyway?' Guy said. 'He might figure out that it's a trick. And you're still putting my daughter in danger just by taking her back to Mallingham.'

'We can't guarantee that and yes, we are putting Katie at some risk. We don't even know that Beckett will agree. But we have to do something. We're running against the clock here. Beckett and his troops have turned up a blank even though they're swarming over Mallingham like a plague of flies. We have to flush him into the open. There's a young boy's life at stake.'

'Ray and I should be with Katie and then with whoever you choose as substitute,' Shaw said. 'Katie's parents too. We have to make Nathan believe that we've gone back to Mallingham and if we're all there then there's a better chance. If Nathan believes it, so will James and they'll both come.'

George nodded. 'I'll get someone to drive me back to town and I'll talk to Beckett.' He nodded apologetically at his empty glass. 'I've had a bit too much to take myself.'

Katie's mother sat back down, staring helplessly at them all. She was close to tears but knew that she too had to agree. 'Katie goes into the hotel and straight back out again,' she insisted. 'Straight out again.'

'I promise you,' George said. 'I wouldn't put her in any danger, Lisa. I know what it's like to lose a child.'

Nathan had kept pace with James. The other one had panicked and his flight had been easy for Nathan to follow.

James had led him towards the twin rivers, across the bridge and to a disused warehouse placed at the point of the headland where the rivers joined. By the time James had gone to ground, Nathan had read two things in James's mind. James was running scared and the boy, the fourth boy, was still alive.

Chapter Forty-Three

Nathan moved through the darkness with a silence and certainty that most people would not possess in daylight. He had returned for his bike, riding to the bridge and then pushing it the remaining quarter-mile. Then he had paused for breath. The Domi was heavy and not designed for hauling over rutted ground. He found a piece of level ground, pulled the bike up onto its centre stand and checked that it was secure, looking anxiously about him, hating to leave the bike so exposed. His only consolation was that the bad weather meant the streets were empty and, unless you knew what you were doing, the bike was hell to kick over. Its high-compression engine gave it a tendency to kick back if you caught it on the wrong stroke. If that happened the kick-start was quite capable of breaking someone's knee.

James had entered the building through the broken door. Nathan took a more circumspect approach. He circled the warehouse slowly and found a place where the old fire escape still looked relatively intact. It had been broken off some eight feet from the ground and Nathan jumped for it, missing twice and scraping his knuckles painfully before finally catching the lowest rung. He hauled himself up with arms that already trembled from the exertion of pushing the bike, trying to keep his thoughts calm and confined, afraid that James might feel how close he was and know what he intended to do.

The fire escape rattled as he swung his left leg over the rung and then pulled the rest of his body after. This was not the way he could bring a child out. He'd have to risk the main door. He moved swiftly up the stairs. One of the fixings had broken free and the landing swung ominously, creaking away from the red-brick wall. He kicked hard at the door, flinching as it crashed inward, then he slipped inside and crouched on the landing keeping very still, hardly daring to breathe in case James had heard.

The silence gathered solidly around him. He waited until he was certain James had not heard and then moved along the corridor and down the stairs. The upper storey had been given over to offices. Desks and filing cabinets had been left behind, papers still strewn across the floor. Nathan glanced swiftly through each door as he passed by but there was no sign of the child. Too high, he thought, too high up for James.

The stairs were concrete, four flights leading to the lowest floor. He travelled as lightly as he could in heavy boots, listening at each turn of the stairs, his mind reaching out for James, trying to pinpoint which part of the building he might be in. And then he heard the child. A soft, muffled whimpering coming from the floor below.

Nathan quickened his pace. He could feel James too now. He was at the far side of the building, as far away from the child as it was possible to go. Nathan slipped through the stairwell door. It hung sideways from a single hinge, half blocking his exit. The child was to his left now. He could hear the muffled cries more clearly, plaintive and distressed, and for a moment he was back eleven years before with the child in the cellar of the Markham house. He found himself looking back over his shoulder, half expecting that Lee would be standing there.

But no. That had been the third victim of Lee's obsession. There had not been a fourth. Lee would not be there this time and neither, if he kept his head, would James.

The child lay on a pile of sacking in what had once been the loading bay, the level of the floor dropped down from that of the main warehouse. He had a blanket draped over him, but Nathan could see that his hands and feet were tied with rope and that his eyes and mouth were covered by dirty rags tied untidily in place. The makeshift gag stopped the child from crying out but not from making sounds and his muffled sobs echoed around the bay.

Nathan moved quietly towards him, but the boy heard and his body stiffened and the cries changed, becoming more alarmed. Nathan knelt at his side and tugged the blindfold free. There was little illumination in the bay. Nathan's eyes had grown accustomed to the dark but the boy blinked rapidly and Nathan realized he could not see anything. 'I won't hurt you,' he whispered. 'Look, I've come to help.'

He reached into his pocket and removed a knife and a torch. Switching the torch on, he lay it on the concrete floor so that the boy could see his face. 'Don't scream,' Nathan warned, 'or he'll come and find us.' He removed the gag and began to cut the ropes that bound his hands and feet. 'My name is Nathan,' he told the boy. 'I'm going to get you home but we must be quiet and we must move fast. You understand?'

The boy nodded, his eyes wide and scared. 'Will he come back? What if he comes back?'

Gently, Nathan placed a finger against the boy's lips for silence. 'Can you stand?'

He eased the child up onto his feet, knowing that the pain of returning blood was going to be unbearable and debilitating. He would have to carry him. He reached down and picked up the torch, then swung the child lightly across his shoulder and began to run back across the warehouse, sacrificing silence, this time, for pure speed.

James burst out of the far room just as Nathan reached the door. With a scream of fury, he flung himself across the concrete distance between himself and Nathan, but Nathan was through the door and running hard, trying not to fall on the muddy, rubble-strewn ground, heading back towards his bike.

The boy was crying now, cold and scared and pained by the blood returning to his hands and feet. Nathan hauled the bike off the stand and swung himself aboard, kicking hard at the pedal, praying that the Domi wouldn't let him down. Wouldn't play hard to get, as these old machines so often could. It took three kicks, the third hitting the compression stroke and throwing his leg sideways before it gave in and roared into life. The boy was screaming, watching James clearing the distance between them and the warehouse. Running madly, slipping in the mud that turned the ground into a quagmire. Nathan hauled the child aboard and took off fast, dropping the clutch too rapidly, the front wheel skidding across the ground.

'Just hang on tight,' he yelled. 'Just hang on to me and don't let go.'

It was advice the boy did not need. He clung to Nathan, fingers clawed around his waist. The bike roared, the sound of the pipes cracking harshly in the damp air. They cleared the bridge and headed back into Mallingham, revs hitting the red line, and it was only when they had put about a mile between themselves and James that Nathan slowed. He headed back towards his old home in the basement, to where he knew there would still be officers on watch. He paused only for the briefest of moments ten feet away from the nearest man before urging the child to get down and thrusting a piece of paper into his hand. And then he was gone, leaving the boy and the two uniformed officers staring after him.

Chapter Forty-Four

By early the following morning everything was in place for Katie's return to Mallingham. News of Marcus Ellwood's dramatic liberation was all across the media, replacing scheduled programmes and filling the bulletins. It was the first break in an otherwise dire situation and a feeling of, in Ray's opinion, unfounded optimism pervaded the police station and Mallingham itself. Ray's worry was that this would force James into action. That he would abduct another child and kill them as quickly as the first ones had died. No one could really understand why he had delayed this time.

All the more reason why Katie's plan must work.

Shaw and Beckett were already at the hotel when Ray arrived. George was to be part of Katie's escort. The manager and his staff had been briefed on a need-to-know basis, being told that this was vital to the investigation but not exactly why their hotel had been taken over by the police.

There were armed police in the surrounding buildings and at ten o'clock Emma Thorn arrived, muffled up in winter clothes. She went straight to what would be Katie's room. Emma was a fraction taller than the girl, a little heavier, but with her blonde hair loose and cut for the occasion the match at a distance would be good enough.

Jane Adams

Ray, being briefed by Beckett, knew that Nathan and James would soon get wind of all this. The manager had to inform his staff. The comings and goings, the discreet police presence, the odd glimpses that the public would get of armed police on nearby roofs, all this was enough to ensure that security would be as leaky as the proverbial sieve – which in this case was exactly what was wanted. Only Katie's departure from the hotel was to be guarded. That was the most important thing of all.

Beckett went on the lunchtime news to issue a statement about the fourth child. Ray watched his performance on the television in the hotel room. Katie sat beside him on the bed, her hands clenched nervously in her lap. She kept glancing towards the window, as though she expected James Morgan to burst through at any moment and drag her away.

'You all know by now that at approximately eleven-fifteen last night Marcus Ellwood was found, safe and well. For the moment we want to keep the circumstances of his recovery unpublicized, but suffice it to say it's the first break we've had in this investigation and we are confident that it will lead to an arrest very soon.' He paused, waving down the storm of questions. 'I can't give you more details. I'm sure you'll appreciate the reasons for that, but Marcus is in hospital, with his grandparents. He was cold and exhausted and, I'm told, very hungry, but he's not been harmed and we're expecting him to be released from hospital later today.' He looked expectantly at the assembled journalists waiting for their new questions.

'Douglas Hemmings, Inspector. The *Mallingham Post*.

Will you comment on the rumours that there has been a further abduction? A young girl by the name of Katie Fellows. She was the child found the night the chapter-house where Lee's lot based themselves was blown up.'

'I can assure you that Katie Fellows has not been abducted,' Beckett said smoothly.

He looked for the next question, but Hemmings was not giving up that easily and it appeared he was not the only one to be onto Katie's story. 'Carter, Inspector. BBC. The neighbours say that Katie's family have been away from their home for several days now and that Mrs Fellows told them Katie had run away. She thought Katie might be heading for Mallingham. Is there a connection between the girl and the dead boys?'

Beckett hesitated for a split second. He had known for some time that this was bound to get into the media. He played it instinctively, knowing that he had to be seen to be giving something. 'We've tried to keep Katie and her family out of the spotlight,' he said, as though reluctantly, 'but yes, it's true that when Katie heard about Lee's death she panicked. You have to understand that Katie was scarred by her involvement with Lee. The man terrified her, threatened that he'd come back for her one day, even if he had to die to do it. Katie really believed that she'd put the past behind her, where it belonged, but when she heard that Lee had died the old fears came flooding back. The girl has been through a great deal, as I'm sure you can appreciate. Her biggest fear was that Lee would somehow threaten her family and she ran away to try to protect them.'

There were murmurs among the crowd. There was

more to this and they knew it, but Beckett wasn't going to give.

'You'll be glad to know,' he went on, 'that Katie is safe and well and has been reunited with her family, though not unnaturally they prefer to keep a low profile until this is over. They've decided to stay with friends for a while until they feel ready to go home.'

There were more questions about Katie, but Beckett ignored them. As he was about to go, though, someone threw a question at him that he could not ignore.

'Inspector, is it true that letters were sent to DCI Bryant warning him that this might happen, but that he chose to ignore the warnings?'

A ripple of interest moved through the crowd.

Beckett turned back and sat down again, knowing that he couldn't get away without tackling this, though truth to tell it had caught him off guard.

'I'd be interested in knowing your sources,' he began. Laughter greeted that and gave him a moment more to think. When he replied, it was with caution and he felt for his words. 'After the first deaths eleven years ago and the arrest of Harrison Lee people within his organization feared that someone else might try to continue. Lee ritualized the murders, though we're still unclear as to his actual intent. Probably only Lee could have told us that and I can assure you all that he never did.

'He boasted, however, that locking him away would not stop what he called his work from going on and Martyn Shaw, when he took control of what was left of the Eyes of God, believed that we should be made aware of these threats.

'I knew nothing about this until two days ago, but yes, DCI Bryant had been warned. At the time, though, eleven years ago, those warnings must have seemed incredible and far-fetched. And DCI Bryant is now dead. I'm sure, had he lived, he would have not hesitated to remind this investigation of these warnings, though whether or not that would have affected our actions in this case I cannot say.'

He rose then and made clear that the press conference really had come to an end. The shouted questions as he walked away told him that the media were far from satisfied. He'd have given a lot to know where the journalist had got his information. It would not have been from Shaw, of that he was certain. But Farrant. Farrant would almost certainly have known about Lee's threats and about Shaw's feeling that he had to warn Bryant.

Would Bryant have talked to Farrant? Beckett wondered. Would Farrant have assured him that this was just Martyn Shaw making yet more trouble? If so and this had been instrumental in Bryant's dismissing Shaw and hiding the fact that he'd been warned, then Farrant could well have cost them far more than just time.

Chapter Forty-Five

It had been decided that Katie should remain in the hotel until late evening to give time for Nathan and James to convince themselves that she was there.

By mid-afternoon Nathan was in the street at the rear of the hotel and wondering what Ray was playing at. He figured it must be some kind of trap for James and felt his anger rising at their risking Katie in this way. He had trusted Ray Flowers, believing he would protect Katie, and now to find that she was back here, exposed and vulnerable again, seemed like an outrage.

He was aware of James moving parallel to him only a street away, hiding himself among the crowds of shoppers gathered for the Saturday afternoon. He was aware also of the police presence, sometimes glimpsed, sometimes just sensed, and knew that James would sense them too, not that it would stop him. James was angry now. He had gone beyond the capacity for reason, long gone. He had imbibed the sanctified blood of the first three chosen and the only thing that puzzled Nathan was why he had not killed the other boy. The one the papers said was called Marcus Ellwood. That afternoon, though, he had figured it out. Katie was to be the fourth, the same as last time. The boys, then Katie, then three more. He had no orders from Morgan to kill the fourth until he had Katie. The pattern had been broken, the taking of the fourth boy so soon mistaken and opportunistic. James had to correct the error.

And the timing was right, Nathan felt, though he could not explain why. It was something James knew, some rule that Lee's spirit told him to obey. James needed Katie, he needed her tonight.

In the hotel the hours passed between tension and boredom. Fear is a hard and tiring thing to sustain and Katie had watched videos with her parents, even laughing at the jokes. At last it was time for her to go. She wanted to stay now, scared of what might happen to her parents or to Emma Thorn, weighed down with responsibilities that had nothing to do with who she was, only with what Lee had believed she might be. She had gone downstairs wearing Emma's coat and hat and thick scarf, and left through the back way with George, the delivery van that was to be her means of escape pulled right up to the hotel door.

In the darkness, Nathan had found a place to hide.

A street away in the door of a closed shop, James felt his presence and was reassured. Nathan wanted to protect the girl. Tonight Nathan would find out just how strong Lee's soul could be.

An hour later, George phoned to say that she was safe back at the house. Everyone else settled back down to wait, satisfied at least that Katie was out of the way.

Chapter Forty-Six

It was Martyn Shaw who first realized that there was something wrong. Since Katie left he had been sitting motionless in one of the armchairs placed close by the curtained window. His eyes were shut and his hands lay still upon his knees. He was meditating, Ray had supposed. Or whatever it was that prophets did. Ray himself lay upon the bed. Too wired to sleep but letting his thoughts ramble and glad his companion was in no mood to talk.

It was some twenty minutes after George's call that Martyn opened his eyes and looked at Ray.

'Call George,' he said. 'Do it now.'

Ray sat up, the urgency in Shaw's voice transmitting itself to him.

'Why?'

'Just do it. Something's not right.'

Ray picked up his mobile. George's phone rang out and then switched to the message service. He tried again with the same result. Then he found the safe-house number that George had given him and dialled that. This time he was routed through Dignan's exchange before his call was allowed to go through. Moments later he was off the bed and heading for the door.

'George never arrived,' he told Shaw.

Within minutes Beckett was mobilizing his people and

the helicopter was in the air following the route the van would have taken from the hotel. Ray stood beside the door, taking in the scene. The hotel room now crowded with people. Katie's parents furious and hysterical, Emma Thorn doing her best to calm them down. Beckett shouting down the phone. He turned to Shaw.

'With me,' he said.

Shaw was gazing into the middle distance, his eyes unfocused, as though he was staring at something very far away.

'Nathan's here. James hurt him, I can feel his pain.'

Ray's look was less than sympathetic. He shouted to Beckett that they were going out, that he had an idea and would call in *en route*. Beckett was too wrapped up to argue. 'Call Dignan,' Ray told him. 'Fill him in. You might need more back-up.'

'Now where's Nathan?' he demanded as he led Shaw from the room. 'And where the fuck has James taken Katie and George?'

'The Markham house,' Shaw said, his tone so certain that Ray shot him a suspicious look.

'This a feeling,' he asked, 'or something more?'

Shaw smiled grimly. 'My feeling was right about George,' he said. 'But it's also logical. Think about it. You've driven Nathan from his home. Nathan gave the child the location of the warehouse, so now it's swarming with police. Where else is there to go?'

Ray nodded. 'It makes sense,' he admitted. It was remote and familiar and if they had possession of the van . . . How many men had George provided? How had James overpowered them? Just what the hell was going on?   -

They did not have to look far for Nathan. He was leaning on Ray's car, blood pouring down his face.

Ray fished the first aid kit from the boot and left Shaw to patch him up, ushering them both into the rear of the old Volvo.

'What happened?' he demanded.

'He hit me with something. I think he thought he'd killed me when I went down. He's got Katie, hasn't he?'

Ray nodded. 'George as well. What the fuck went wrong, Nathan?'

'You're asking me? You stupid bastards set this up.'

He sighed, leaning back in the seat and allowing Martyn Shaw to clean the long wound on his head.

'He should be in hospital,' Shaw said.

'When I've got a minute I'll drop him off. Tell me, Nathan, what did we do wrong?'

'You gave him Katie. You brought her down into the street just where he was waiting. He's not stupid, Ray. You all thought, oh, he's just some psycho, some poor, disturbed, unthinking moron. You don't realize, do you, any of you? James isn't stupid and he isn't blind. He knows and feels more than any of you lot ever will. He might not live by your rules, you might not understand him, but he's being guided by Lee's soul and he's got complete faith in that. He doesn't care who or what he has to go through to make this thing work, because he doesn't see it. Any of it. He doesn't act as if it's there and so it's not.'

Ray shook his head. 'I don't get you, Nathan. There were armed men in that van.'

'You don't shoot at smoke,' Nathan said wearily. 'Or if you do, you miss, and I doubt James ever gave them time.'

George had known that something was wrong before he set foot inside the van but by that time it was far too late. James had Katie and a knife, already slick with blood, was held across her throat.

'Drive,' James said. 'Just drive and don't think I won't kill her, now or later, it's no different to me.'

Katie's eyes were wide in panic and George knew that nothing he could say or do would make this easier for her. He could smell the sweet heavy scent of blood filling the delivery van, he could smell shit and guts. He was just relieved that the carnage he could well imagine was in the rear and Katie could not see it.

George got into the driver's seat. James guided Katie into the seat alongside him, not taking the knife from her throat. He positioned himself behind her, wedging himself against the body. 'Now, I told you to drive,' he said. 'It doesn't matter where, just away from town.'

George started the engine. Outside the crowds had gone, the rain had returned and there was little traffic on the road. The police on the roof would not be able to see who was driving, only that there were two people in the front as expected, and with the knife unflinchingly held at Katie's throat he knew that there was nothing he could do.

'They'll be expecting a call, won't they?'

George nodded. 'In about an hour's time.'

'Then make it, when I tell you, and keep it straight or you both die.'

'I thought that was the option anyway,' George said mildly, and immediately wished he hadn't as he heard Katie whimper and begin to cry.

'You're making it worse for her,' James said. He lifted his other hand and used it to stroke Katie's face, his fingers tracing the curve of her cheek and the softness of her hair. 'I've waited a long time for this,' he whispered. 'A long, long time.'

Lee's spirit within him had never felt so strong.

No one had spoken much on the drive to the Markham house. Nathan, concussed and pained, lay back on the seat trying to get his thoughts together and Ray, driving far too fast on country roads, had little concentration to waste on Shaw beyond telling him to call Beckett and tell him where they were headed.

A quarter of a mile from the house he caught sight of the van, partially concealed in a stand of trees. He braked hard and backed up, then ran from the car to investigate.

Shaw was beside him when he opened the rear doors.

'Oh, my God. Are they both . . . No, Ray, one of them's alive.'

He was right, Ray realized as he scrambled into the van. The floor was slippery with blood and when Ray touched the walls to steady himself his hand came away red.

'There's a torch in the back of the car. Get it, then

call Beckett, tell him we need an ambulance. Tell him no sirens.'

Shaw ran back to the car. He returned with the torch and the first aid kit. Ray took them both and crouched over the wounded man. He had been stabbed in the gut, three or four times as far as he could see. He pressed padded bandages against the wounds, applying as much pressure as he could. The man groaned in pain as he bound the wounds. Ray knew it was probably too little too late and marvelled that the man was still alive. His colleague was dead. His throat cut. In the torchlight it looked like a single cut, no hesitation, severing his neck almost as far as the spine.

Shaw climbed in beside him and held the torch, giving Ray a better view of the surviving man's wounds. It was well meant, but Ray almost wished he hadn't bothered. The light made everything look ten times worse. The man's eyes were rolling in his head and though Ray spoke to him he seemed unable to respond.

'Can I do anything?'

'I don't know, can you? Do your super-powers run to reviving the dead?'

'I never tried. The ambulance is on its way. I've told Beckett no sirens. How close are we, do you think?'

'Don't you take offence at anything? Look, I'm sorry, I didn't mean . . .'

'Not much these days. And I know you didn't. I'm not a healer, Ray. I never claimed to be. What do we do now?'

'I don't know. We can't leave him. How long before Beckett's people get here?'

'He reckons no more than twenty minutes. He says you shouldn't be playing the hero.'

Ray calculated swiftly. 'Stay here. Look after him and when Beckett arrives bring him to the Markham house. Katie might be dead by now.'

'She's not,' Shaw asserted confidently. He smiled. 'My super-powers *can* tell you that.'

'I hope you're right.'

Ray slid back out of the van and crossed to the car, shaking Nathan awake. Nathan groaned.

'Listen. It's you and me right now, that's all we've got, so get yourself together.'

He waited impatiently while Nathan stumbled from the car. One fat ex-cop and one concussed sociopath, Ray thought, the flash of humour rising unbidden to his mind. Not much against some guy convinced that he was God.

George had never been to the Markham house but he guessed from the road that they were taking that this was their destination. It was the first glimmer of hope. Ray or Shaw or even Beckett might guess that's where James would take them. Then he remembered that no one yet knew that they were missing, so no one would be trying to guess where they were.

An hour to the minute after leaving the hotel James ordered him to pull off the road and make the call. George could see his watch in the faint light shed by the telephone screen. It was eleven-fifteen. George did as he was told, telling Emma Thorn, who answered the phone, simply that Katie was safe and they were at the house, hoping that she would notice something wrong or that at least she would deliver his message verbatim and they might think it curious. He thought of risking asking to speak to Ray, but one look at Katie's face told him not to. The girl was white, colour drained even from her lips, and her breathing was shallow and uneven. Katie was dead already in her own mind. He knew then that he would have to play this for both of them. There was no hope of her collaborating with him or following his lead. No hope that her nerve would hold, especially if he seemed to be pushing James where he did not wish to go, or even of negotiating. Katie would interpret that as further threat, George was certain. He was in this alone.

'Put the phone under the seat, then drive,' James said, and George did as he was told.

They reached the Markham house somewhere towards midnight. George had lost track of time and it was too dark to see his watch. James had him pull the van off the road and then get out of the cab. The rain had stopped but it was pitch, heart-of-the-country black with no moon and hidden stars. Had he been alone or with someone like Ray, George would have risked acting, attacking James as he came around the side of the van, but he was with a sixteen-year-old child, he reminded himself. He doubted that she would run even if he managed to free her.

It was about a quarter of a mile to the Markham house. George hoped for traffic, but there was none, the road leading nowhere except the village in one direction and the crossroads in the other, both a couple of miles distant.

They reached the gates of the Markham house and went inside.

'Back there.' James nodded, after taking his bearings. 'Back there towards the trees. Go now.'

George led the way from darkness into even deeper black. The trees of the Markham site closing in around them and blocking out the sky.

Ray could hear their voices. George was speaking quietly and Katie was crying, her sobs soft and almost animal in their confused hopelessness.

He could hear James, chanting it seemed, though Ray could not understand the words. His voice was too soft and the words said too swiftly. The relief that they were alive was overwhelming, he had anticipated coming to the house and finding them both dead. In his journey he had found himself rehearsing the words that he would say to Katie's parents when he told them that their child would not be coming back.

Nathan was beside him, crouched by the gate, listening intently. 'Man is like an angel falling,' he whispered softly. 'That's what he keeps saying. Over and over again.'

'Now we wait for Beckett,' Ray said, but Nathan shook his head.

'Lee,' he whispered. 'I can feel Harry Lee all around this place, all around them. Lee's controlling him, Ray. He's going to kill her, there's going to be no time.'

Ray turned to look at him. 'I don't believe all that.'

'Believe it, just for now, because that's the way it works. Lee's telling him to get this done. To do it now and then go on with the other boys. He's furious with me Ray, and if we don't move now . . .'

Ray hesitated for a moment more and then he nodded. 'That way,' he gestured. After all, there was only one James. He tried not to think of the two men in the van.

Ray circled the overgrown garden, keeping low and close to the hedge. He could hear George's voice more clearly now, talking to James, his voice steady and calm, though Ray could hear the underlying fear.

'It's not too late to back down, you know. You're not acting by your own will, James. You're being controlled. We know that and we care about you. We want to make this right again. James, you don't have to go through with it.'

Ray could see them now. James was kneeling on the grass, one arm circled around Katie's waist as she knelt in front of him, her body pressed close against his own. Her head was thrown back and resting against his shoulder, the position determined by the knife James was holding at her throat. Her little cries were growing weaker. Her hands rested on his arms as though she tried to control him, but his body was rigid and far too strong, and Nathan was right, Ray observed, James was taller and more heavily built than the slight young man Lee had chosen when James had fallen apart.

George had moved, crouching, his body tense and ready to act should the opportunity arise. Across the clearing at the rear of the ruined house, Ray could just see Nathan, a deepening of the shadows, moving slowly, inching his way towards the frozen tableau with Katie at its centre. But he too was afraid to go further in case the knife should move just once across the girl's exposed throat. One almost thoughtless progression would be all it would take. Ray thought about the man he had seen, his throat cut almost to the bone, and knew that James was more than capable. He had not killed the last boy because the timing wasn't right, that was all, not out of any sense of mercy. And from the other boys Morgan had needed living blood if this ritual of his was to work. Apparently Katie did not meet the need in the same way.

Then Nathan moved. A sudden rush of blackness detaching itself as it had on the night he had attacked Ray. He moved with such speed that Ray's eyes could not follow him, and as he moved he cried out words that Ray could not understand, and as he moved past, Ray felt that sense of otherness that he had experienced on the night all those years ago when he had watched the old man die.

But James felt it too. He shouted, an inchoate cry, and whirled to face Nathan's sudden attack. Coming to his feet with Katie still clasped in his arms.

George rose from his crouch, attacking from the side, his hands grasping at the knife that James still clasped in his fist. James turned on Nathan, shaking George aside as though he were nothing, and Katie fell sideways, knocked over by George's rush and James's sudden turn.

Ray grabbed her. She was bleeding, he could feel the

blood on his hands. 'I'm all right. I'm all right,' she
gasped, and he pushed her into the cover of the hedge
and turned back towards the fight. He had heard descriptions of prisoners on PCP taking out a dozen officers
before they were finally brought down. He didn't know
what was possessing James, but whatever it was the effect
was much the same. He and Nathan were wrapped in an
embrace so close it might almost have been obscene.
George was struggling to pull Nathan free, or maybe
James away from him, Ray wasn't really sure.

Behind him he felt Katie move, and when she rose up
beside him she had James's knife clasped in her hands,
was wiping the blood from the handle on her clothes and
thrusting it into his grasp.

'In my dream,' she yelled. 'You stopped him in my
dream.'

Ray took the knife, staring stupidly at her, and then
he leapt forward. James's arm was wrapped around
Nathan's throat and Ray plunged the knife deep into his
bicep. He plunged it in and then pulled it down as James
screamed and tried to escape. He sliced into muscle and
felt the hardness as he hit the bone. And then he snatched
it out again, looking for another place to strike.

Nathan had fallen now. He lay on the ground, clutching at his head. George had his hands wrapped in James's
hair and was hauling backwards, trying to pull him
down. Ray struck again, the knife this time sinking into
James's leg. He felt inspired, that was the only word he
had for it. He didn't need George's help now, he could
take this bastard down all on his fucking own. He
wrenched the knife from the man's leg and raised it up to

strike again and then there was a flash of pain, the pain spreading from his hand and up his arm.

Ray lay on the ground, the inspiration spilling from his body, suddenly aware of figures all around him, moving past, surrounding him. And Beckett kneeling at his side with a uniformed officer holding a night staff in his hand.

'He hit you,' Beckett explained. 'I'll get him to apologize some time.'

'James Morgan?'

'We've got him. It's going to be all right.'

Ray lay back, allowing the pain in his hand and arm to expand until it filled his consciousness. It felt good, the pain, real and solid, something he could understand in a world that he would swear had all but gone mad.

It was some time until they realized that, in the confusion, Nathan had gone.

Chapter Forty-Seven

The blow had broken Ray's wrist, but he didn't care. A few weeks in plaster seemed a small price to pay. What stuck most clearly in his mind through the following days and weeks was the feeling that he had wanted so much to kill James Morgan that for a few precious minutes it had been his only reality.

He had never experienced such cold, inspired rage before and it shook him that such a feeling was something he might be capable of.

Katie was alive. Marcus Ellwood was alive – and back in school. James Morgan was in hospital, in a secure unit, and Ray doubted he would ever be judged fit enough to stand trial. Martyn Shaw had returned home and Mallingham to its sense of bleak normality . . . and Beckett had come up with a theory.

'Morgan,' he had declared. 'Morgan didn't die in the chapterhouse explosion. Morgan had to be behind all of this. He controlled his son before and he's controlling him now, maybe even killed the boys.'

It had a sort of logic to it and the search for Daniel Morgan had begun, though Ray doubted they would ever find him, and even if they did that they would be able to prove his influence over his son's actions.

They were also searching for Nathan, but Ray was even more certain that Beckett would fail in that. It would be like catching smoke, to borrow Nathan's description of James, and Ray was glad of it. He couldn't bear to think of Nathan locked away.

It was two weeks after the shocking events at the Markham house that Ray saw Nathan. Ray was with Sarah in Mallingham, visiting Martha at St Leonard's Church, when they all heard the distinctive note of the Dominator. They turned and looked across the wasteground to where the body of Roger Joyce had once been found and saw Nathan on his red and chrome machine. He looked at them for a moment and nodded at Ray and then took off into the night carried on a wave of noise.

'Will you tell Beckett?' Martha wanted to know.

'Tell him what?'

Martha smiled.

That I saw a fallen angel, Ray thought to himself as he walked away.

LIMERICK COUNTY LIBRARY